*"I do n… …uren,"
Emiliano … …you will give
me no choice if you refuse."*

"So you're giving me no choice instead?" Bitterness
tinged her voice as she struggled with his ultimatum.

Another movement of an eyebrow said it all.

As she'd already pointed out, he was rich and
powerful. He could tear her heart out if he wanted
to. *And he probably wanted to!* she thought acridly.
Instead he was offering her ecstasy. Physical ecstasy
in return for not taking Danny away from him.
Unbelievable physical ecstasy. And a suitcaseful of
self-degradation when it was all over.

"All right. I'll accompany my nephew," she told him with
her voice cracking. "To look after him and make sure
that where he goes and what he does is in his best
interest. But if you think that you and I will be picking
up from where we left off two years ago, then you've
got another thing coming! I won't be your plaything,
Emiliano. Not now or at any time in the future."

D1115912

All about the author...
Elizabeth Power

ELIZABETH POWER wanted to be a writer from a very early age, but it wasn't until she was nearly thirty that she took to writing seriously. Writing is now her life. Traveling ranks very highly among her pleasures, and so many places she has visited have been recreated in her books. Living in England's West Country, Elizabeth likes nothing better than taking walks with her husband along the coast or in the adjoining woods, and enjoying all the wonders that nature has to offer. You can visit her at www.elizabethpower.net.

Other titles by Elizabeth Power available in ebook:

VISCONTI'S FORGOTTEN HEIR
A GREEK ESCAPE
A DELICIOUS DECEPTION
BACK IN THE LION'S DEN

Elizabeth Power

A Clash with Cannavaro

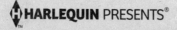

HARLEQUIN PRESENTS®

Recycling programs
for this product may
not exist in your area.

ISBN-13: 978-0-373-13245-4

A CLASH WITH CANNAVARO

First North American Publication 2014

Copyright © 2014 by Elizabeth Power

Printed in U.S.A.

A Clash with Cannavaro

To Alan—remembering our lovely days in the Caribbean.

CHAPTER ONE

LAUREN RECOGNISED THE man as soon as he stepped out of the car, a shining silver monster of a thing that looked incongruous against the rustic outbuildings of the Cumbrian farmhouse and the verdant slopes of the fells above its wet slate roofline.

It was the man striding across the yard with his hair blowing like an untamed mane in the wind that her gaze was fixed on, however, as she finished securing the stable door for the night.

Tall, lean, in his early thirties, his expensive tailoring could do nothing to conceal a physique honed to prime strength and unquestionable fitness, or those shoulders which were wide enough to eclipse the moon. But he was a man she had never expected—or hoped—ever to see again, and she watched his approach now with a leap of something electric lighting her wary green gaze.

'Hello, Lauren.'

If she was lost for words, then it was only because she was shocked to see him there on her Lakeland property. A property on which her late parents had blown all their savings to chase a dream of self-sufficiency—a dream that had never quite lived up to its promise and which was a world away from the glamorous capitals of Europe and the far-flung playgrounds of the mega-rich that the man before her inhabited.

'Emiliano!' She could have kicked herself for sounding so breathless and for wishing that she was wearing something other than her vest top and dungarees, or even that she had had a chance to comb her hair. After being out in the damp air, checking on the horses she stabled for the few paying customers who helped subsidise her meagre income from the local garden centre, she knew the flaming waves were falling untidily about her shoulders in a blaze of ungoverned fire. 'What are you doing here?'

A definite wobble weakened the challenge in her voice. But then it wasn't every day that she found herself facing Emiliano Cannavaro, Italian shipping magnate and steel-hard billionaire. The man who had taken the already international freight and ferry line his grandfather had founded and turned it into a global giant, spearheaded by a fleet of luxury cruise liners. A man who had used his Continental charm and his chocolate-rich voice to lure her into his bed, only to discard her in the most degrading and humiliating way after the marriage of her sister, Vikki, to his younger brother, Angelo, two years ago.

'We have to talk,' he said.

She had forgotten how tall he was, and how, without the benefit of high heels, she only just reached his shoulder. What she hadn't forgotten was how it made her stomach flip just to look up into his olive-skinned features—features that had been redeemed from being too handsome by that slight bump in his nose, and by the glaring virility in that clean-shaven, yet heavily shadowed angular jaw.

She cupped a hand over her eyes to shield them from the low evening sun. 'What about?' Her tone was accusatory as she did her best to ignore the effect his sudden appearance was having on her.

'About Daniele.'

Eyes fringed by lashes only a shade darker than her hair regarded him suspiciously. 'Danny?' Her voice cracked as she felt the burn of his hard masculine scrutiny over the flushed, perfect heart shape of her face.

With unsettling thoroughness he was taking in her rebellious green eyes, small chin and slightly turned-up nose with its cluster of freckles that her mother used to say was a sprinkling of stardust, before his gaze dropped with unconcealed insolence to her mouth. It was a full mouth, usually marked by a natural curve, but at this moment was definitely hinting at mutiny as his eyes came to rest disconcertingly on hers again.

His assessment made her feel weak, but it seemed to have no effect on him whatsoever as he gestured towards the ancient farmhouse and said, 'Shall we go inside?'

Inside? Together? Alone? With him!

Her heart-rate doubled its pace. 'Not until you tell me what this is all about.'

'All right. If you want it straight. I would like to see him.'

'Why? When you haven't come near him or even rang to enquire after his welfare in over a year?'

If she wasn't mistaken, Lauren heard him catch a breath. So he was feeling guilty. Good! she thought, cutting him no slack.

'If I have neither telephoned nor been to see him,' he responded with the firming of a mouth too sensual for any woman of child-bearing years to possibly ignore, 'it is because you allowed none of us to know where he was.'

Lauren stared at him incredulously. 'Is that what your brother told you?' she exhaled, flabbergasted. 'Or is that something you dreamed up yourself? Anyway, I didn't think he mattered to you. Or to any of you Cannavaros,' she expanded bitterly, recalling how his brother had as good as disowned his six-month-old son only weeks after Vikki's death nearly a year ago. Still walking with the aid of a stick because of the injuries he had sustained in the car crash that had claimed her younger sister, Angelo Cannavaro had informed Lauren in plain, insensitive words that she could keep the baby her sister had used to trap him into marriage because he was cutting loose. That was the last time she had seen him. Or any member of the Cannavaro family! Though it had hurt her immensely for Danny's sake, she couldn't say that she hadn't been relieved. And now here was Emiliano Cannavaro turning up and accusing *her* of being the one at fault! 'You've got a nerve!' she breathed.

He raked his hair back from his forehead with a long, lean hand. Hands which, in one weekend, had learned the pathways of her body and the whereabouts of every erogenous zone she possessed. His face was harder than she remembered, although even back then it had been a face stamped with authority, with a high forehead and cheekbones clearly defined. Add the midnight mystery of spectacularly dark eyes, thickly arched black brows—one of which was lifting now as

though in dispute of what she had accused him of—
and long ebony lashes that most teenage girls would
probably have killed for, and she could see why she
had been rendered helpless from the moment she had
laid eyes on him.

'As I suggested, could we go inside?'

His tone brooked no argument and so without a
word she led him across the yard and in through the
back door of the rugged little farmhouse, uncomfort-
ably aware that he was probably enjoying a studied
view of her back and the curve of her bottom and remembering...

'So say what you've got to say.' A strong sexual
awareness made her tone excessively curt as she
rounded on him in the large but shabby kitchen. But
the memory of how this man had bedded her and then
treated her as if she wasn't even fit to tread the same
ground as he did never failed to shame and humiliate
her—even without suddenly coming face to face with
him and having to relive it all over again!

'As you wish.' He didn't seem at all perturbed by
her unfriendly manner. 'I shan't...What is the term you
use? Beat about the bush?' Nevertheless, he seemed to
hesitate for a second before continuing. 'You are probably aware that Angelo died just over a month ago.'

She nodded. She had been shocked to read about it
in one of the national newspapers. Accidental death,
the verdict had been. Caused by a lethal mix of strong
painkillers he'd been taking for his continuing back in-
jury and an excessive amount of alcohol in his blood.

Lauren was sorry, but all she could say right then
was, 'So what does that have to do with me?'

'Everything,' he answered succinctly. 'Because,

from now on, this monopolising of Daniele is going to cease.'

'I haven't been monopolising him!' she shot back. 'At least, not intentionally. But if I have, it's only because your brother took no interest in him whatsoever, which is one of the reasons Vikki left him.' Among others, she thought with a mental grimace, before adding, 'And neither have you.'

'Something I fully intend to rectify,' he promised. 'But as I have already told you…' he was beginning to sound impatient '…I did not have the first idea where Daniele was. As you probably…remember…' his hesitation was marked, calculated, Lauren was sure, to remind her of an intimacy she didn't even want to think about '…I live in Rome. But on those occasions when I visited this country, Angelo assured me that Daniele was being adequately cared for. It was only a short time before he died, when I put pressure on him to tell me where he was, that he said he had left Daniele with you and that he didn't have a clue as to where you had taken him. Why would he have told me that if it was not true?'

'Because he didn't want you to know what the truth really was!' Lauren returned hotly.

'And exactly what is the truth, Lauren?' Emiliano invited, in clearly sceptical tones.

'That he abandoned Daniele because he couldn't face the responsibility of being a father! He knew exactly where I was and how to find me. He could have come any time to see Daniele and I wouldn't have stopped him,' she fumed, hurting for her little nephew. 'But he didn't because he didn't want to give up his gambling and his womanising and everything else about the self-indulgent high life that both of you enjoy so much!'

It was a cry from the heart at the injustice of what both her and her sister had had to pay for getting mixed up with the Cannavaro brothers. Heaven knew, Vikki hadn't been any saint! But she hadn't deserved the drunken abuse and infidelity that had forced her into leaving Angelo after less than ten months of marriage. Any more than she, Lauren, had deserved his brother's scorn and bitter contempt...

'Nevertheless,' Emiliano said coldly, seemingly oblivious to her indictment of self-indulgence or to the pain that seemed to be turning her inside out, 'Daniele *is* his son, and therefore my nephew.'

'And you naturally want to see him.' She had to concede that much. As the toddler's natural aunt and uncle they were equal claimants for the little boy's affections. Even so, she took some gratification out of being able to say, 'Well, I'm afraid that it's not going to be possible tonight because he's already asleep.'

She sensed the tension in him and for the first time noticed the dark smudges beneath his eyes, caused, no doubt, by the recent loss of his brother. But then he gave the slightest tilt of his head, causing his hair to fall forward again in the way she remembered it doing. Somehow it seemed to emphasise the satanic darkness of his shadowed jaw.

'I understand,' he said, surprisingly compliant all of a sudden. 'But I do not think you do, Lauren. You had, however, better know from the start what my intentions are and to be fully aware that I will be demanding much more than that.'

A queasy feeling took root in the pit of Lauren's stomach. 'Wh-what do you mean?' she asked cagily.

'The boy is a Cannavaro. Therefore it is only right that he should be with his family.'

'He *is* with his family!' she proclaimed, her face flushed with indignation to think he could even suggest anything else.

He was glancing around her kitchen, which she knew had seen better days with its chipped Belfast sink and genuinely distressed oak table and matching Welsh dresser that stood against the far wall, and he looked at her now with something remarkably like censure shaping the hard line of his mouth.

'You think it fitting for a child of his background to be brought up in a place like this?'

His deprecating opinion of the home she had once shared with two loving parents and her sister cut Lauren to the quick, but she was determined not to let him see.

'So it isn't the mansion that *you* obviously think he should be living in,' she bit back, fearful of what he intended to do about Daniele. 'But, with respect...' this last word was overlaid with sarcasm '...he'll learn more above love and basic human values in this shabby old house than he'll ever get to know in the sterile palaces your sort of people call home!'

Whether she had hit a nerve in his invincible armour, or whether it was just her audacity in speaking to him as she had that put that flush across his cheekbones and made his jaw tense as though he was clenching his teeth, Lauren wasn't sure. But she was struck by the vivid recollection of seeing him look like that before. It was the second before he had driven into her hot and eager body and had finally succumbed to the release of his, until then, frighteningly controlled passion, taking her with him on a mind-blowing excursion to a fool's heaven!

'And what would you—or your sister—have learned about basic values?' he challenged softly, as Lauren battled with spiralling and unwelcome sensations from remembering how it felt lying naked beneath this man's warm and penetrating strength.

'Nothing, according to you,' she replied, with only the slightest quiver in her voice. Because, of course, he hadn't listened to any explanation when he had labelled her and Vikki the worst kind of women, so there was no way she was going to try and convince him otherwise now, especially when he was adding child abduction to her sins as well!

'And what do you imagine is my type of home?'

Strangely, she had never been able to place him anywhere, other than in the swish resorts where the rich and famous vacationed, or in some stark, state-of-the-art high-rise office at the heart of his maritime empire.

'I don't intend wasting any unnecessary thought over it,' she retorted, wishing she wasn't letting him reduce her to the level of sniping.

'Not even to wonder where this nephew—whom you claim to be instilling with your own questionable values—is likely to be living?'

Lauren forced herself to bite her tongue. She was past caring over the last two years what Emiliano Cannavaro thought about her. Memories might shame, but they couldn't hurt her. She had learned to shrug her shoulders, grit her teeth and carry on. But Emiliano Cannavaro wasn't a memory any more. He was here—

now as large as life, and he had it in his power to hurt her and would if she let him, by taking away the one thing she held most dear.

'I don't need to wonder, Emiliano,' she said determinedly. 'I know exactly where he'll be living. And that's with me. It was my sister's wish that I should take care of Danny if anything ever happened to her before he became of age.'

'Which she had no right to express or to request of you while the child's father was still alive.'

'She had every right!' Lauren shot back, affronted by his dictatorial attitude. 'Although she wouldn't have needed to if Angelo hadn't been as bad a father as he was a husband!'

'You mean the husband she saw only as the key to a life of luxury? And one she had no intention of giving up?'

I'm going to screw him for every penny I can get!

Lauren didn't want to remember Vikki's venomous remark on that tragic day, eleven months ago, when her sister had gone off to see Angelo, leaving the six-month-old Danny in Lauren's care. But it came back startlingly now with the things Vikki had told her on her wedding day, things that Lauren wished—if only for her own sake—that she had never heard.

'Oh, don't misunderstand me.' The deep Latin voice penetrated her thoughts, bringing her back to the present. 'I am not defending Angelo's actions.'

Lauren slanted a censuring look at him. 'Aren't you?'

'My brother's faults were glaringly obvious, but that didn't stop him from being totally and utterly taken in.'

Which you never would be, she thought, skimming

a reluctant glance down over his magnificent physique, and shuddering as she recalled the way he had reacted when he thought he had been.

Those dark assessing eyes of his seemed to be stripping her naked with their unsettling intensity.

'No,' he said, in a way that was lethal in its very softness, startling her into wondering if he had the power to read her thoughts

'No what?' she challenged, trying not to think about that day that had been the most humiliating of her life.

He didn't answer.

He didn't need to, Lauren thought, with colour tingeing her cheeks.

'I did not come here to resurrect anything that might have transpired between us,' he remarked coldly. 'Though, heaven knows, if there had been a prize for driving a man crazy you would have won it hands down, would you not, *mia cara*?' His tone made a mockery of the endearment. 'You did not exactly hold back in your efforts to please me that night I took you to my bed.'

How she could feel a throbbing deep inside just from thinking about that night, Lauren didn't know, and shaming colour stained her cheeks almost puce.

Somehow, though, she managed to say cuttingly, 'Save it, Emiliano.'

He laughed, savouring her discomfiture and embarrassment like he'd savoured the nectar of her willing body.

'Of course. There are far more pressing matters in hand.'

Like taking Daniele away from her?

'If you think I'll be handing my sister's baby over to you just like that, you've got another thing coming!'

He smiled, the type of smile that had had the power to draw her to him that fateful weekend two years ago in a way she had never been drawn to any man before or since.

'Of course, I would not be expecting you to hand him over—as you say—"just like that". Naturally there would be a period of adjustment while the child became acquainted with me as his new guardian. And naturally you will be suitably rewarded for the time he has been in your care.'

Dumbfounded, Lauren couldn't believe what he was saying.

'Suitably rewarded?' She flung the words back at him as if they were poison darts. 'And what is the price you'd consider *suitable* for trading a child?'

A dark eyebrow shot up as he regarded her with something approaching disdain.

'I am not buying him from you, Lauren, if that is what you're imagining. I will simply be reimbursing you for the inconvenience and loss of earnings you will most certainly have suffered during the time you have been caring for him. But if it means that much to you, I will allow you to name your price. Within reason. I am sure that between us we can arrive at a figure that will suit us both.'

'Oh, are you?' Disbelievingly, Lauren stared up into the strikingly masculine face, trying not to baulk at the determination she could see stamped on every purposeful feature. 'You think you and your kind can buy anything you want, don't you? Well, sorry to disappoint you, Emiliano, but I've no intention of giving up my nephew any time soon. So you can take your fancy car and your over-stuffed wallet and go back to whatever cold, damp stone you happened to crawl out from under, because Daniele isn't going back with you under any circumstances! Not now. Not ever!'

His mouth twitched at one corner as he contemplated what she was saying. 'And there I was thinking that we could be civil about this,' he remarked. 'Do I understand you to be saying you would prefer a legal battle?'

And one he would surely win?

Tremulously, yet refusing to be fazed, she answered, 'If that's what it comes to.'

He clicked his tongue. 'You are very foolish, Signorina Westwood.' The formality only seemed to widen the glaring distance between them. 'It seems I underestimated you in imagining we could come to a reasonable settlement without resorting to the needless involvement of expensive lawyers. Or does the idea of a court case whet your appetite for a taste of even greater pickings?'

'You're despicable!' Lauren breathed.

'Not nearly as despicable as you would find me if you drag me through a court of law.'

She looked at him askance. 'Is that a threat?'

'No, just some good advice.'

'Well, you can stick your advice where the sun doesn't shine!'

He laughed very softly. 'Such spirit!

He was moving towards her and she backed away, sending a shocked glance over her shoulder when she came up against the solid bulk of the dresser.

Hardly daring to breathe, she stood stock-still, her

eyes guarded and challenging as Emiliano's hands came to rest on the dresser on either side of her, effectively trapping her there.

'You know…that was the first thing that attracted me to you. Other than…' One strap of her dungarees had slipped off her shoulder, dragging the bib down with it, and from the slide of his gaze over the vest it had exposed she knew he could see the outline of her naked breast. Breasts which were too full, she had always thought, in comparison with her small waist and far less curvy hips. Now, in response to his heated gaze, she felt the nipple swelling beneath the soft revealing cotton. 'The way you tried to cut me dead in response to everything I said was a real turn-on. And it was not just me who was affected by it, was it, *cara*?'

He meant her, Lauren thought with shame, remembering how he had even gone as far as suggesting that she actually enjoyed arguing with him.

'And that was even before you knew who I was.'

The softness of his voice and his nearness was making her head start to swim. She hated him! And yet it was taking all her willpower not to thrust out her breasts in invitation to those hands that had pleasured her like no other man ever had.

But she didn't. And thankfully he didn't attempt to touch her.

Instead, straightening up, with his face taking on grim lines, he said, 'May I also advise that if you take me to court and you lose, then you will get nothing from me. Is that clear? Not a cent.'

'That's good,' she returned, pulling up her strap, relieved at least to be able to breathe again. 'Because I don't deal in cents. Only common decency! Unlike you Cannavaros. But then you don't ever think about anything else except making money!'

'Which is marginally more commendable, I think, than being one of life's takers,' he remarked with an unperturbed, humourless curl to his devastating mouth. 'Nevertheless, where agenda-armed little vamps are concerned I find that it is always best to be one step ahead.'

'So you insult me with the promise of some disgusting pay-off!'

He sent another cursory glance around him at the obvious decay of her clean yet humble environment. 'You look as though you could use it.'

'Not half as much as I could use you getting off my property!'

'Of course.' Though he had stepped away from her now, the fresh masculine scent of him still lingered in her nostrils. 'But I will be back. You can depend on that. And when I do return, I will see my nephew. Is that understood?'

He looked so commanding that for a moment Lauren could only nod. 'I wouldn't *dream* of trying to stop you,' she riposted as soon as she found her voice.

'In that case...I will see myself out,' he said, obviously satisfied that he had achieved what he had set out to do, which was to scare her silly with his threat to take Daniele away from her.

Well, if he wanted a fight, she would give him one! she thought, calling on all the powers of survival she had had to engage as a teenager after losing both her parents. After all, since Vikki had died, Daniele was all she had, and Emiliano Cannavaro could swing before she would give up her little nephew to him or anybody else!

But the fear had taken hold and she couldn't shake it off. And that wasn't the only thing unsettling her as she listened to his powerful car growling away.

It was that raging sexual attraction that had flared into life the minute she had seen him again, coming across the yard. But, even worse, her body's betraying response to it when he had had her trapped—without even touching her—against the dresser. An attraction, she thought hopelessly, which had been born in her the instant she had laid eyes on him across that crowded ballroom, and reluctantly she let her thoughts drag her back to those two days in that exclusive London hotel two years ago.

CHAPTER TWO

WHEN HER SISTER had invited her to her pre-nuptial party on the eve of her marriage to one of Italy's most eligible bachelors, Lauren hadn't envisaged spending what felt like hours smiling politely at a twice-divorced ageing Romeo of a banker until her face ached.

She'd been renting a bedsit in London at the time, having leased the farmhouse for some extra income with a view to going back to college and doing some serious studying. But she had felt as out of place in the city, she remembered, as she had in the emerald-green strapless gown she had been wearing at that party which, with no long-standing boyfriend to accompany her, she had chosen to attend alone. That still hadn't stopped her from feeling immensely relieved when another guest had finally claimed the Romeo's company.

Her sudden isolation, however, had left her exposed to the gaze of a man she hadn't known then was Emiliano Cannavaro, although she had sensed him watching her for most of the time that she had been suffering the older man's unwelcome attention.

With a clear field between them after the banker

had moved away, Lauren had been unable to avoid meeting the cool intensity of his midnight-dark eyes.

He must have been around thirty then and was, from his tanned skin and thick black hair that flopped forward at the temples, like a number of the guests, unmistakably Italian. Yet, in this man she hadn't known, Lauren had sensed an air of cool detachment and authority that had set him apart from the rest. Perhaps it had been that autocratic nose and the way that intensely dark shadow around his jaw had added something to its angular strength that had given her the notion that he wasn't a man to be messed with. Or perhaps it had been that restless quality about him and the rather bored suggestion that he would rather have been somewhere else. But what he had had was presence. And it had been nothing less than spell-binding! Add that impression of straining muscle beneath the constraints of his dark tailored evening suit and Lauren had realised why every woman who had passed within ten yards of him seemed to fall over herself with the need to be noticed by him. And he hadn't taken his eyes off *her* once!

Unused to being studied with such blatant interest, Lauren had looked quickly away to where the reed-slim blonde with the baby doll face and her far too handsome groom-to-be had been standing by the buffet tables with their arms interlinked in front of them, sipping from tall flutes of champagne.

'Is that envy I see in your eyes? Or are you wondering, as I suspect you are, whether they are as happy as their animated laughter suggests?'

The heavily accented voice at her shoulder made every nerve sharpen in Lauren's body, causing her fingers to tighten around the stem of her own glass. But it was the way its rich tones washed over her like a warm wave that had her catching her breath as though she had been submerged beneath the power of its sensuality.

'Why shouldn't they be happy?' The effect of his nearness produced her unusually curt rejoinder. Nevertheless, her eyes challenged his, even though she knew her cheeks were probably as red as her swept-up hair that the woman in the store where she had bought her gown a few days ago had said would complement the emerald creation superbly.

'Why, indeed?' Up close, he looked even more stupendous than he had from a distance. His features were strong with clearly defined cheekbones, and his mouth, she recognised at once, had a hard-edged sensuality that could probably drive most nubile women mindless just from the promise of its unquestionable passion. His winged collar looked stark white against the hard bronze of his skin and he smelled good too, of some subtle masculine cologne that Lauren wanted to inhale—and keep on inhaling—until her suddenly starved senses were full of him. 'She must have something very special to have brought Angelo Cannavaro to heel.'

Unaware that he was the brother of her sister's fiancé, it was the fact that he was obviously acquainted with the groom's playboy reputation that prompted Lauren to ask, 'Are you a friend of the family?'

That passionate mouth of his twitched slightly before he said, 'I would not exactly…call myself that.'

A business associate then, she speculated silently,

and wondered, as she still did, at the reason for that definite hesitation in the way he said it.

A burst of laughter brought her attention to the couple, who were twirling to imaginary music with their arms still linked, champagne flutes still held high.

'She strikes me as a young woman who knows what she wants and exactly how to get it.'

The man's gaze was resting on the obvious mound of Vikki's middle beneath the smoky blue satin of an outrageously low-cut, backless dress, split almost from hip to hem. But the critical note in his voice made Lauren bristle and look up at his devastating profile with narrowing eyes. 'What are you implying, exactly?'

His thick hair gleamed darkly as he turned back to her again. 'No implication, I assure you. But she must obviously be aware that there are worse fates than linking up with one of Italy's oldest and most... significant families.'

Lauren's hackles continued to rise. 'And there are some who might say she could do better than marry into a family which has put too much emphasis on making money at the expense of investing the right kind of values in its offspring.'

Her piqued rejoinder brought a speculative curve to his mouth. 'With you being one of them, I suppose?'

She hadn't intended to make such a pointed remark about the groom's family. It had slipped out before she could contain it, but his comments had irked, especially as she had been so worried about Vikki.

Ever since they had lost their parents within days of each other to that tropical disease six years ago, Lauren had found herself at eighteen playing mother and father to her often difficult and rebellious sixteen-year-old sister. Vikki had reacted to her parents' death by lashing out at the world, and her anger and resentment at their loss had resulted in a spiralling lifestyle of alcohol-fuelled all-night parties, illegal drugs and far too many one-night stands.

Painfully, Lauren recalled how Vikki had refused to listen to her concerns about her ruining her life and eventually, when Vikki was still only seventeen, their differing opinions and clash in personalities meant they could no longer remain under the same roof and Lauren had seen very little of her sister over the next few years.

When Vikki had telephoned only three weeks prior to that party to say that she was not only pregnant, but getting married, Lauren had been as surprised as she'd been happy for her sister. She'd also had to secretly admit to feeling more than a little relieved.

It wasn't until the sisters had met for a tearful reunion lunch that Lauren had learned of Vikki's choice of husband, and her gratitude that her wayward sibling was finally settling down had dissipated on a surge of anxiety.

Angelo Cannavaro's decadent lifestyle was legendary, with his penchant for glamorous women exceeded only by his wealthier, yet considerably more discreet older brother, who, by some miracle, had managed to keep himself and his personal life out of the papers! Which was why Lauren hadn't instantly realised who he was on that first meeting. It hadn't surprised her, though, to learn that Vikki's year-long involvement with the twenty-five-year-old Italian playboy, whom she'd met while working as a croupier in a London nightclub, had already been a tempestuous on-off affair, with Angelo sounding rather too partial to his freedom, in Lauren's mind, to make suitable husband material. Vikki had said he had changed since their last break-up only five months previously, but it had done very little to allay Lauren's worries for her sister's future.

'It isn't for me to cast aspersions on either the bridegroom or the calculating little blonde who's so *lucky* to have him marrying her.' She was unable to keep the sarcasm out of her voice as she clutched the glass she hadn't remembered draining so tightly it was in danger of shattering. 'And neither should you.'

Her reprimand, instead of shaming, seemed merely to amuse him.

With a smile touching his sensuous mouth, he allowed his gaze to stray with disturbing intensity over the fine symmetry of her face, down her rather flushed throat to her full breasts, which were pushed up enticingly—too enticingly, she remembered now with a sensually inspired little shiver—above the shimmering emerald of her bodice.

'And who are you,' he enquired in that remarkably sexy voice of his, 'that you jump so readily to the defence of the blushing bride-to-be?'

She found him so disconcertingly male that it was an effort to meet those equally disturbing eyes with any confidence, but she managed it. Just.

'I'm Lauren Westwood. Her sister.' She gleaned a wealth of satisfaction from saying that.

'Ah!'

'Yes,' she added smugly before he could say another thing. 'Another of the money-grubbing Westwoods, as you've obviously labelled my sister. From one of the most *in*significant families in Cumbria.'

If she had expected to embarrass him then she should have guessed, Lauren thought now, that men like him weren't easily—if ever—caught out. A mere dip of his head in almost amused acknowledgement confirmed it.

'A gross error on my part, I think,' he said, which was as near to an apology as Lauren knew she was likely to get. 'In which case, you will at least allow me to get you another drink.'

'No, I don't…' she started to say as he relieved her of her glass. But the accidental touch of his fingers against hers robbed the words from her mouth as a bolt of something electric ignited powerful impulses in her blood.

His smile was far too aware.

Though not inexperienced, having had a couple of undemanding relationships in the past, she was still unaware of the dangerous responses she was provoking in such a sophisticated man as Emiliano Cannavaro. She took advantage of the remarkably sudden appearance of a waiter at his side to try and stabilise her senses as he deposited her empty glass on the silver tray.

'Insignificant is definitely not a word I would apply to you, *signorina*.' He was looking at her—not in the leering way a lot of men looked at her because of her far too voluptuous figure, but with the subtlety of a man who was well acquainted with the female anatomy and knew just how to turn it to his advantage.

And how! Lauren remembered now, resenting the way he had made—and could still make—everything that was feminine in her respond readily to the pull of his flagrant masculinity.

'Nor I you.' A raw sexual tension made her tongue cleave to the roof of her mouth. 'But then you know that already.' She meant it as a barb, reluctant to acknowledge how those eyes that seemed to be penetrating the emerald silk made her breasts grow heavy. But her voice sounded husky from imagining what it would be like to feel those long tanned hands pulling down her zip, and that sensual mouth moving over the screamingly sensitive flesh covering her spine before…

She brought her thoughts up sharply as her nipples swelled inside their strapless cups.

'What are you doing, Lauren Westwood?' Through a rush of shaming heat she caught the sensuality in his lowered tones. 'Trying to ensnare me with those heavy, come-hither eyes as your sister has ensnared poor unsuspecting Angelo?'

She felt herself blushing, certain that he was fully au fait with her body's shaming responses.

'As you've already pointed out,' she returned, mortified, yet trying to maintain some degree of equanimity, 'Angelo Cannavaro's far from poor. And if you think pledging one's troth is a form of penal servitude then you have a very cynical view of love and marriage!'

'Touché,' he said softly, 'but I wasn't talking about a mutual exchange of vows. There are more ways of being ensnared than by just slipping a ring on one's finger. And it has nothing to do with love…' he seemed to place an almost derisive emphasis on the word '…or even liking.'

Lauren's body pulsed with the need to retaliate in

some way. Because she didn't like him! She thought it
now with as much vehemence as she'd tried convincing herself on that night. Why, then, she remembered
wondering, did her breasts ache to feel his touch? And
why did the thought of pushing him to the limit and
provoking what she guessed would be a frighteningly
controlled yet lethal anger have her playing all sorts
of outrageous scenarios in her mind? Like tumbling
down onto a bed beneath him and quelling their mutual antagonism in the most heated and primeval way?

'I can assure you that nothing is further from my
mind so, rest assured, you're perfectly safe.' She
flashed him a falsely bright smile, yet knew from the
almost indiscernible lifting of an eyebrow that he had
picked up on the breathless note in her voice.

'I don't know whether to be gratified or disap-
pointed to hear it.' His smile was cool and mockingly
sensual. 'The question is, Signorina Westwood...are
you?'

His meaning was so subtly explicit that Lauren was
shocked to feel a deep answering throb in her lower
body.

'I don't know what you're...' Talking about, she
started to say, but her sentence was cut in midstream
as Vikki Westwood, all gleaming teeth and voluminous blonde hair, suddenly exploded onto the scene.

'Oh, great! I see you two have already met. Are you
going to let on, Emiliano, as to what you think of my
sister? Isn't she gorgeous?'

'She is.' Vikki's words seemed to give those dark
eyes licence to tug with leisurely insolence over Lauren's shamefully aroused body. 'But I'm afraid we
haven't yet been properly introduced.'

'Emiliano, this is Lauren, my older and very available sister. Lauren, this is Emiliano Cannavaro. *The* Emiliano Cannavaro,' she emphasised with relish. 'Angelo's older brother and the head of the Cannavaro dynasty—not to mention the company—since their father died last year.'

Lauren recalled her dismay at finding out that the man she'd been as good as insulting was the one man her sister had previously warned her to be nice to. She was already cringing from the way the younger girl had pointed out her unattached status to him, without being made aware of exactly at whom she had been directing her uncharacteristically barbed remarks.

'He flew in from Rome to join us tonight and for the wedding tomorrow, even though he's so busy and it was such short notice and he only touched down less than two hours ago. Wasn't that good of him?' Vikki added unnecessarily, although her rushed and effervescent sentence went some way to explaining why Lauren hadn't noticed him earlier in the evening. 'But don't be fooled by all that Italian charisma and irresistible charm because, from what I hear, he doesn't suffer fools easily. He might look like the perfect gentleman and like a gift from the gods to all womankind but, from what Angelo tells me, he'll break you if he can. Snap you in half.' She clicked her tongue and made a meaningful gesture with her hands. 'Like a twig. So mind how you tread, lovely sister.' Lauren detected a thread of nervous anxiety in her sister's warning and in her shrill little laugh. 'Oh, well. Better circulate. See ya!' And with that she spun away in a cloud of expensive perfume.

Mortified, Lauren watched her sibling grab another

female guest's arm, saw several air kisses being exchanged.

'I hope you don't think that my sister's outspoken remarks have any bearing on my character,' Lauren remarked, still recoiling from the way Vikki had referred to her as 'available'.

'Meaning?' Emiliano sent her a slanted look.

'Why didn't you tell me who you were?'

'You didn't ask,' he rebuked her softly, unfazed by the censuring note in her voice. 'Why? Would it have made any difference to our conversation if you had?'

She considered his question for a moment. *Yes, it would*, she thought. *I would have run like the wind before it took the turn that it did!*

'I thought not,' Emiliano expressed with that mocking twist to his lips, misunderstanding her hesitation in answering.

'Is it true what she said?' She looked up into eyes that were much too dark to be anything but sinful. 'That you break people?' She recalled wondering why his own brother would say a thing like that.

Something pulled at the corners of his arresting mouth. 'Is that what you would like to believe?'

He was much too worldly—way out of her league— and Lauren prayed he hadn't noticed the way her throat worked nervously before she replied, 'No, but I think you could.'

She didn't know why she had said that, but all he did was throw back his proud dark head and laugh.

'I am afraid that your sister, as you are probably well aware, is rather a drama queen. Isn't that what you English call it?' And when she nodded, he told her, 'I do what is necessary. But I am always fair.'

Strangely, she believed him. From what Vikki had already told her about him, he could run rings around his brother for playing hard and fast. As brothers, they weren't that close, but Vikki had sounded overawed when she'd spoken of the respect Emiliano's leadership had generated among his colleagues as well as his employees, and Lauren had only been able to guess from the success of the company that it had the right man at its helm. After all, Cannavaro Cruise & Freight Lines were up there with the kings of the seas.

Changing course, she asked, 'Why aren't you best man?' She'd already chatted earlier to the person who was taking on that role and he'd been an old college friend of the groom's.

Emiliano's mouth tugged down at one side. 'It's a long story. Why aren't you maid of honour?'

'It's an even longer one.'

Something almost feral flickered in those sinful eyes. 'I've got all night.'

She should have listened to the warnings leaping through her, Lauren thought bitterly in hindsight, because all her instincts of self-preservation had been urging her to shake off the sensual spell that Emiliano had woven around her ever since he had come over to speak to her, but she hadn't seemed able to move, nor had she wanted to. But neither had she felt inclined to tell him about the past strained relationship with her sister, or what had brought it about, and so she'd evaded the issue altogether by saying, 'I didn't come here tonight to bare my soul to a perfect stranger.'

Perfect being the operative word, her brain had whispered provocatively.

'My brother is marrying your sister,' he reminded

her. As if he needed to! 'That surely relates us in some obscure way.'

She caught sight of herself in a mirrored pillar and noticed how her hair seemed to blaze like luminous fire. Or like the ultimate scarlet woman's, she thought with a kind of feverish excitement as she glanced quickly away.

'Even relations have secrets from each other,' she parried with a smile, trying to avoid thinking too much about the estrangement between her and Vikki. But, in doing so, her words came out with unintended provocation and she saw the heavy masculine eyelids droop as his gaze sliced over her body.

'In that case, we will not dwell on it a moment longer. So what would you like to tell me?'

'That you speak very good English.'

He looked amused again. 'So do you.'

'I should think so!' she told him, amazed. 'I'm English!'

Laughter lit his spectacular eyes as he said, 'Believe me, *mia cara*, the two do not necessarily go hand in hand.'

Lauren laughed with him, feeling more relaxed than she had since she had first arrived in the hotel late that afternoon with her weekend case containing her gown and her outfit for Vikki's big day.

'Tell me, beautiful Lauren…' The way he addressed her sent peculiar little shivers along her spine. 'Is it because your sister warned you what a tyrant I can be—and therefore to treat me amiably—that I now feel the ice melting around my feet?'

'No. I never listen to or act upon anyone else's opinion of someone without first weighing up their character for myself,' she told him candidly. 'And if you're mistaking truthfulness for frigidity then you're in danger, Emiliano Cannavaro—' she experienced a surprising thrill in saying his name '—of finding yourself in very deep water.'

'And you, Lauren, are a very smart lady and especially refreshing. But I think perhaps that you actually enjoy crossing swords with me.'

It wasn't far from what Lauren had been thinking earlier when she had imagined them locked in sexual combat in some not so imaginary bed. A throb of tension made itself felt again, deep down inside of her, which was wholly sensual and totally out of character for her to feel with a man she had only just met.

'You blush, *mia bella*.'

'It's hot in here,' she prevaricated, which brought another smile to his lips because it wasn't hot at all. In fact the hotel's air conditioning system ensured the temperature remained comfortably cool.

'There is, of course, a remedy for that.'

'Which is?' she asked cagily.

His eyes indicated the floor to ceiling doors that stood open onto the terrace.

'You expect me to wander out into the moonlight with a man I don't know and might not even care to, and whose reputation I'm sure precedes him, if some of the speculation I've read about you is to be believed?'

'It isn't,' he responded succinctly. 'And you are wrong.'

'There is no moon,' she amended, because she had been speaking only figuratively.

'So no silent witness to judge such decadent behaviour.' He laughed then, his teeth showing strong and white against his tan. 'Unless, of course, you are afraid...'

She uttered a tremulous little laugh. 'Of you?'

Was she? she wondered, with her breathing quickening, wishing now that she had listened to her instincts. But he had been merely a fellow guest at her sister's pre-wedding bash and, after that, Vikki's brother-in-law.

That description of him mocked her with its banality. In no way did such an ordinary word fit the man whose persona seemed to energise the very air around her and whose nearness sent coils of excitement spiralling through her blood.

So why didn't she just take a chance? she asked herself. Have some fun for once, instead of always being the 'sensible' one, as her parents used to call her? The one who was level-headed, cautious and careful—both in her behaviour and in her everyday living—always working hard and keeping house, first for Vikki's sake and then, after Vikki had stormed out, simply to keep a roof over her own head. She didn't imagine that it could possibly hurt her to take some time out and simply let herself go for a few short hours. And if she and Emiliano had started off on the wrong foot just because of what he had said initially about Vikki and Angelo being happy...Well, she decided, talking herself round, it was no more than she had been wondering herself, was it?

So she allowed Emiliano to lead her outside and remembered now how much they had talked and laughed, sitting there under the stars on the low wall of the softly litterrace, wrapped up in their own world, with the music from the ballroom drifting towards them, although she remembered very little afterwards of what had been said.

It had all been a prelude to what they had both known was going to happen, and even before Emiliano's lips came down over hers it was already too late.

Now, in bitter retrospect, she saw that night only as a prelude to shame and humiliation, but out there, on that terrace, all she had been able to focus on was the excitement of Emiliano's hands shaping her body and the sensations that were governing her, making her shudder with need from the warmth of his mouth moving over her bare shoulders and the way his deep voice trembled from his own desire.

She didn't want to think about that exquisite night—because it *had* been exquisite. As was the following morning, she recalled reluctantly—waking up in his bed in that hotel with little enough time to get ready for the wedding, and yet answering his hungry demand with a rising hunger of her own as he'd pulled her back against the hard excitement of his scorching arousal.

She could scarcely remember how many times he had taken her since she had yielded to that first blazing kiss on the terrace, but she'd taken him into her that morning with a body already fashioned by his will, her luscious breasts surrendering to his hands and his burning mouth, her legs fanning open without any further persuasion to accommodate the driving force of his body.

Even while she had stood in a demure cream dress and fascinator at her sister's wedding she had been on fire for him, with her breasts swelling against the lace of her bra every time she thought of him. She remembered wondering with a sort of guilty excitement if everyone could tell just how she was feeling, and if her cheeks looked as flushed as she felt they did from the excited anticipation of what lay ahead, because Emiliano had made no secret that morning of wanting to keep her in his bed.

She hadn't had much chance to speak to him during the register office ceremony or during the lavish reception, when they had been seated at opposite ends of the table back at the hotel. Then, afterwards, when everyone had been mingling, he had been monopolised by so many people who wanted to talk to him that she had kept her distance, appreciating how important his role as head of Cannavaro Shipping was, and how sought after his attention was by many of the guests. Also, with Angelo being part of such an influential family, the press had been very much in evidence all that day. Remembering how much Emiliano valued his privacy, Lauren had guessed that if he was keeping his liaison with her low-key, then it was only to protect them both from speculating reporters.

The day had been drawing in and they had barely spoken at all, but the glances he'd sent her way when he'd looked up occasionally over the head of whoever had been monopolising his company at that moment assured Lauren that he wanted to be with her as much as she wanted to be with him.

She was in love. Or halfway towards it!

Like a fool, she had almost convinced herself of it while she had been waiting for her sister—whom she'd presumed had gone upstairs to change before she and Angelo left for their honeymoon—to come back down.

With Emiliano engaged in conversation with a couple of younger men who had been hungrily absorbing every word he had been saying, Lauren had wandered off to steal a few moments to herself in the peace of the luxuriously deserted lounge, out of range of the noise of the ballroom.

Only it hadn't been deserted.

Still in her wedding dress, Vikki Westwood had been studying her reflection in the huge mirror above the sculpted fireplace. The mirror faced the doorway and, as soon as Lauren entered the room, she'd noticed the surprisingly anxious expression on her sister's face.

Emiliano's words of the previous evening had come sharply back to Lauren's mind and, with them, the worries she had been harbouring about her sister.

'Vikki…What is it? You are happy, aren't you?'

Her sister swung round, obviously startled to see her there.

'Of course I am,' she said, and her face was instantly lit by a radiant smile. 'It's just junior starting to kick. Why would you imagine otherwise?'

'It's just that it's all so sudden,' Lauren recalled saying. 'This wedding. The baby. I mean…are you absolutely *sure?*'

'Believe me. I know what I'm doing,' Vikki stressed.

'It's just that you've never been too keen on the prospect of motherhood…' Lauren remembered how often her sister had positively rebelled against it.

'Not just for motherhood's sake, no, I haven't. But I can learn to be maternal. And what better way than with a handsome and exceedingly rich husband beside me?' She giggled and the voluminous hair bounced against her flushed porcelain features like golden candyfloss.

'I just think I would have been happier if you'd

waited a little while longer before starting a family. Got to know each other a bit better. Enjoyed a year or two of just being there for each other.'

'For heaven's sake, Lauren! That's so old-fashioned! But then you always were. And naïve, if you don't take umbrage from my saying so.'

'Naïve?' It hurt Lauren to think that she and her sister weren't able to see eye to eye, even on that day of all days.

'You don't think that all this...' an expansive gesture of her arm indicated the lavish wedding celebrations '...would have happened if I hadn't forced Angelo's hand and engineered this pregnancy, do you?' She laughed out loud at Lauren's silent disbelief. 'Don't look so shocked, sister dear. After all, you can hardly claim to be any different, can you? I saw the way you were cosying up to that big, big brother of his last night, and the way the two of you disappeared after you went out onto the terrace. Did you manage to talk him into bed?'

'Vikki!'

'No, don't tell me. I can see you did. I'll bet he's a real super stud between the sheets!'

Lauren could still remember the embarrassed indignation she'd felt at Vikki's remark, which made her cheeks burn with flaming colour.

'Wow! That good, eh?' Vikki enthused. 'A bit hotter than that lascivious old banker I thought you were trying to land yourself with last night,' she went on when Lauren was still trying to come to terms with how devious her sister seemed to have become, 'until, of course, you saw the opportunity to set your cap at some serious money. I'm proud of you, sis. I really am. I didn't think you'd have the courage to play for such high stakes as Emiliano Cannavaro, but your street cred's really gone up in my estimation. Play your cards right and you could have it all there. Wealth. Position and—from the look of you—some stupendous sex as well.'

'Vikki!' Lauren found her voice at last, but she wasn't prepared to discuss what had happened between her and Angelo's brother. 'We're not discussing me. It's you I'm concerned for. What did you mean about engineering your pregnancy? Surely you didn't…'

'Leave off the Pill and get pregnant on purpose? How else did you imagine I was going to get that confirmed playboy bachelor to propose? Five months ago, when we got back together after that last break-up, I made up my mind that things were going to be different. Such a rich, handsome package seldom comes a girl's way more than once in a lifetime, and I was determined not to let it slip through my fingers again. But don't you see…' her tone was emphatic, excited, animated '…if you've hit it off with his dynamo of a brother, it's all working out as we planned.'

Lauren frowned, so appalled and perplexed by what Vikki was saying that she was dumbfounded, lost for words.

'OK, so you haven't hooked Emiliano yet, and if he's anything like his brother he'll probably run a mile if he thinks you're trying to. But play your cards right, sexy sister, with that demure smile and that stand-offish attitude that always has them straining at the bit, and that big hunky beast won't know what hit him. He might think he's in control, but he'll just be putty in your hands.'

The cliché jarred, especially when it was her, Lauren, who had been like putty in Emiliano's hands. But the things her sister kept coming out with had become more and more outrageous.

'Vikki, I can't believe—' she started to say, only to have her reprimand curtailed by Vikki's swift interjection.

'That I still have the list?'

'The *list*?' Lauren's confusion was so complete that those two words escaped her on what sounded like an almost hysterical little laugh. But she didn't want her sister to think that what she was saying was funny. It wasn't funny at all.

'Our list of possible candidates. Most suitable husband material. These two Italian playboys were always at the number one spot.'

Voices outside and then the appearance of another guest looking for the rest rooms silenced whatever Lauren had been about to say. But, as soon as the woman retreated, Lauren launched into a tirade that left her sister in no doubt at all about how she felt.

'If you think I condone your behaviour, Vikki, then all I can say is you're very much mistaken, so please don't try and include me in your unscrupulous actions. Quite frankly, I'm appalled! How you could be irresponsible enough to let yourself get pregnant when you don't even want a baby is bad enough. But that you could do it to trap Angelo into marrying you is not only devious but downright immoral and, quite honestly, it's beyond anything I would have believed you capable of stooping to.'

She went on to remind her sister that their dream of marrying Italian millionaires was something they'd entertained as young adolescents and which she'd thought they had both relinquished—because *she* certainly had—as soon as they'd grown up!

Her sister warned her that she was part of the very influential Cannavaro family now and begged her not to tell anyone, least of all Emiliano. 'He could be lethal if he thought anyone was double-crossing him—or any member of his family,' Vikki told her in a rising panic before going on to add, 'And I do love Angelo. I really do!'

Lauren couldn't remember what she had said to her sister after that. Only that she'd watched unhappily as Vikki and her new husband had climbed into the taxi on the first leg of their Turkish honeymoon, with Angelo fielding bawdy comments from a number of his bachelor friends and Vikki smiling brightly through a shower of confetti, looking every bit the perfect couple on their perfect day.

Lauren hadn't imagined she could feel any worse than she did at that moment, in not only having quarrelled with her sister on her wedding day, but having to carry the disturbing knowledge of Vikki's deception as well. But when she'd gone back into the hotel and virtually collided with Emiliano, striding through Reception with his briefcase and his features as grim as a rock face, she'd felt her spirits plummet to new depths as she uttered the first words that sprang to her lips.

'You're leaving?' It had been pretty obvious that he was.

'What did you expect, *mia cara*?' His tone clothed the rock face with sheer ice. 'That I would stick around and be made a fool of as my brother has? Is that what you were hoping? Exactly how many times did you imagine you could sob out my name before I would crack and you could mark up one big beautiful tick against your *list*?'

Stunned by his coldness and by exactly what he had said, Lauren was only able to stand there and utter breathlessly, 'You *heard*?'

'*Sì, cara.* I heard,' he rasped.

'How?' It was all she could say, hurting not just from that scene with her sister, but from Emiliano's harsh and very inaccurate conclusion.

'I don't really think I need to tell you,' he said grimly. 'I came to find you to ask if you would have dinner with me tonight, and all I can say now is that I am very glad I did. If I hadn't, who knows what sort of sucker you might still have been taking me for, but, thanks to the conversation I overheard between you and your opportunistic sibling, I was able to see quite clearly what game you were playing.'

'It wasn't a game.' Dear heaven! she despaired. How could he even think so?

'Emiliano!' Desperate to make him understand, she called after him as he made to depart. 'How could you believe I could be party to anything that Vikki said?'

'Very easily.' He'd stopped, but his tone was inexorable. 'If I remember correctly, you sounded no less than positively amused.'

She tried to protest—tried to pinpoint what might have given him reason to think she was amused by anything that had transpired during that scene with her sister, but she couldn't think straight, let alone remember.

'If you recall, I didn't exactly fall over myself to

get you to notice me—talk to me,' she reminded him lamely. 'And I certainly didn't give you the come-on once you did.'

'Not until you knew who I was. But wasn't the stand-off all part of your clever technique? And it worked, did it not? Even your own sister commented on your doing so well? After all, there is nothing more challenging to a man than to be rebuffed by a beautiful woman in whom that man is more than mildly interested. Nice try, *mia bella*. But I have no intention of being a pushover on some little fortune-hunter's list.'

It was no good trying to convince him that that list had been the product of a bit of fun on a wet Sunday afternoon, drawn up by two overly romantic adolescents when she was sixteen and Vikki fourteen, because he wasn't in any mood to listen. Vikki had done enough with her outrageous revelation to destroy his opinion of both of them.

'It's been…nice,' he told her with sickly emphasis. 'I am usually not partial to weddings. But thanks for the diversion. You made the whole tiresome charade quite…' his gaze tugged over her breasts and a mirthless smile touched the hard line of his mouth '…unforgettable.'

Then he went, leaving Lauren feeling as ashamed and degraded as he had intended.

Ten months later, Vikki's marriage had ended and she had left her Hertfordshire home with Daniele to stay with a friend. The following month she had crashed her car during a blazing row with Angelo, when she'd been driving him back to his own car after a lunch meeting to discuss their divorce.

Only a matter of weeks later, after that upsetting

visit from Angelo, Lauren had moved with Danny from her cramped little bedsit, back to the farmhouse, and, until today, had never seen or heard from Emiliano Cannavaro again.

CHAPTER THREE

COMING OUT OF Heathrow Airport, Emiliano congratulated himself on having had a successful week.

A dispute between the management and electrical engineers that had threatened to delay the launch date of Cannavaro Lines' newest cruise liner had been resolved. Shares over the company as a whole were showing record levels. And only that afternoon he had finalised negotiations for the takeover of a European passenger ferry line, which had been on the table for some time now. All in all, he thought, as he stepped out into the dreary greyness of an English autumn afternoon, he felt justified in flying off to his private retreat and taking the break he had been promising himself for a long time—and with only one hurdle to jump. He intended to take his nephew with him.

It was pouring with rain as he set off on the long journey northwards, his car's powerful tyres cruising through the spray as they covered the miles in the fast lane of the busy motorway.

He knew he should have telephoned Lauren to let her know that he was coming, but he hadn't, and for a very good reason. When he had spoken to her from his Rome office earlier in the week to advise her of his wishes, they had been met with fierce opposition. There had, however, never been any problem he couldn't overcome, or any challenge he couldn't meet, but the most difficult, he'd learned from an early age, were often best dealt with head-on.

No one answered when he knocked on the door of the farmhouse several hours later and, going around the back, he found the rear door slightly ajar.

A toddler's tricycle was abandoned in the little lobby to the kitchen, he noticed as he allowed himself to go through, calling her name.

Again, he was struck by the poor conditions she was living in, which were a far cry from the chic modern flat he'd imagined the woman he'd met at his brother's wedding called home. He still couldn't quite equate the glamorous creature who had set out to seduce him two years ago with the tousle-haired, natural-faced, but nonetheless desirable female he had confronted when he had driven up here over a week ago, because there was no doubt that he still found her desirable. More so, if that was possible...

His heart kicked over as he heard footsteps on the flagstones in the hall beyond the kitchen. A woman about the same age as Emiliano, with dark hair tied severely back in a ponytail, strode in, balancing a toddler on her hip.

The child surveyed him solemnly before his gaze skittered past him, over his shoulder. 'Lauren...' The little face seemed to crumple in disappointment when it was obvious that she wasn't there.

'Who are you?' the woman demanded, looking him up and down. She was wearing corduroys and a thick check shirt and looked as though she wouldn't take any messing from anyone.

Quickly, Emiliano introduced himself, before enquiring after Lauren.

'I'm afraid she's out,' the woman told him with a refreshing indifference on hearing his name.

Unlike Lauren, who had come on strong to him when she had found out who he was, he reminded himself, bristling, as again his eyes took in the jaded furnishings, the cracked plaster on the ceiling and the dark patch in one corner that signified definite damp creeping up the wall. No wonder she had been out to get her clutches into some rich fool at that party! he thought, unable to forget how she had been all smiles for that other man she'd been chatting up before she'd obviously decided it would be more to her advantage to make a play for *him*.

A little hand reached out to touch the dark blue stripe in his tie and a shaft of some complex emotion sliced through Emiliano as he took in the brown hair and surprisingly blue eyes of the child. His brother's child. He couldn't help catching the tiny hand in his.

'And you are Daniele.' He wished with every power he possessed that he could take the little boy with him immediately. That his brother hadn't been as foolish and uncaring as to leave the child with his aunt—if she was to be believed—so that he could have brought him back into the Cannavaro family legally, and without all the hassle that he found himself facing now.

'Want Lauren!' the toddler told him pointedly.

You aren't the only one! he thought, and decided that the sooner he took his nephew out of this damp and dreary place, the happier he would be.

'I'm afraid he doesn't like leaving her side for a moment,' the woman who had introduced herself as Fiona told him more amiably now, as she hoisted the child further into her arms. 'But I'm afraid that you, young man, are coming back with me tonight as your mother has an appointment first thing in the morning. I was hoping she'd be in before I left,' she said, clearly worried, to Emiliano, before explaining briefly to him where Lauren had gone. 'She should have been back...' awkwardly, she consulted her watch behind the little boy's back '...long before this.'

It was on the tip of his tongue to tell her that he was the child's uncle and therefore she could leave Daniele with him. He knew she would probably cave in if he pressed hard enough. But the little boy didn't know him and he didn't want to cause him any unnecessary distress. Apart from which, he needed to talk to Lauren alone.

'Why don't I simply go and look for her?' he suggested, sensing that wherever this brusque but frank-speaking woman was taking his nephew, she was more than keen to go.

A few moments later, armed with directions, he was back in the comparative luxury of his car, with his headlamps cutting through the deepening murk.

'It's all right, boy. I'll get you out of this,' Lauren said soothingly to the Border Collie that was lying at her feet, although deep down she was beginning to despair.

The sheepdog, ever friendly, had followed her from the farm but, distracted by a movement in the field running alongside the lane, he had dived through a hole in the barbed wire fence and managed to get himself tangled up in the lethal wire.

She only hoped that the driver of the car that had suddenly screeched to a halt in the lane behind them might have seen them and recognised the plight they were in. She sent an urgent glance over her shoulder as she heard the car door slam.

'Emiliano!'

He was the last person she had expected to see angling himself carefully through the broken fence in his dark business suit, and her immediate relief that someone was coming to help was replaced by a swift, unwelcome tension.

'Your babysitter was getting worried about you.' He straightened as he came through, his hair already misted by the relentless drizzle, and, glancing up at the heavy mist that was coming down over the fells, he said, surprising her, 'So was I.'

She couldn't meet his eyes, dropping hers to his polished slip-on shoes which were more suited to a boardroom than a boggy field.

'Fiona's my stable manager,' she corrected him. 'She looks after the horses for people who have them in livery with us.' As well as being a good friend and stepping in to help with Daniele whenever Lauren needed her. 'I just lease out the stalls.'

'I see.'

The dog wagged his tail, despite his predicament, as Emiliano squatted down in front of him, without a care for his beautifully pressed suit trousers. The scent of his cologne drifted towards her, playing havoc with senses already in turmoil.

'It's all right, boy,' he placated, patting the animal's

head, echoing Lauren's words of a few minutes ago. Reluctantly, though, she sensed that now everything would be all right as he began to help her carefully unwind the wire from around the dog's middle.

'How long has he been like this?'

Beneath her thick damp sweater, Lauren shrugged. 'About half an hour. He followed me, as he always does, but he saw a rabbit in this field and came through that gap—' she jerked her chin towards the gaping hole behind the tangle of vicious wire '—and there was no way I could leave him like this.'

'So who is Stephen?' He didn't look up as he asked it. 'I was informed that you'd gone to see him at the Manor.'

She felt the urge to challenge why he wanted to know. After all, it wasn't as if they had ever been an item, was it? she thought bitterly. But she didn't, answering instead, 'Stephen works in the dairy where I get my milk and eggs.' And was fifty-three with a wife and four children, she thought, but wasn't sure why she kept those facts to herself. 'And the Manor is what everyone around here calls the Home Farm. Why?' she queried, and was unable to stop herself tagging on, 'Did you think I was fancying my chances with the local gentry? Because I couldn't get you?' Then she wished she hadn't added that last bit because it sounded too much as if she was harbouring some romantic feelings for him. She regretted it even more, feeling foolish, when he didn't even deign to give her a reply.

'I told you I wasn't prepared to let you take Danny out of the country,' she reminded him, suddenly fearful that he had come to do exactly that.

'You did,' he agreed, with his thick hair falling over

his forehead as he concentrated on easing the last few barbs away from one muddy black and white foreleg.

His fingers were long and gentle, yet strong and capable too. Hands that had stroked and caressed and excited her like no other hands had ever done...

'There. I think that has sorted you out, boy.'

Freed at last, the dog scrambled to his feet, and Lauren was glad of the distraction from her disconcerting thoughts as he tried to shower gratitude on Emiliano, who was grinning as he dodged the over-zealous canine tongue.

Gently examining the dog as best she could for any wounds that might need medical attention, before satisfying herself that there was no real harm done, Lauren picked up the carton of milk which she'd fetched from the farm earlier and discarded on the ground and then, grabbing the animal's collar, steered him through the metal gate that Emiliano had just opened, patting the dog's rump as she told him, 'Go home now, Brutus. Go on!'

When the dog finally obeyed, loping back towards the farm, Lauren glanced at Emiliano. His hair was glistening with droplets of fine rain. There was mud on the front of his shirt beneath the immaculate jacket, and one downward glance showed that his black shiny shoes were now muddy too.

'Oh, *no!* You've snagged your sleeve!' A thread had been pulled in the expensive fabric of his jacket, just beneath his now not so immaculate shirt cuff.

'It is only a suit,' he stated laconically, closing the gate, which was nothing compared with freeing a painfully trapped animal. Was that what he was saying?

She preferred to think he'd meant that he had more

designer suits than he could possibly hope to get his money's worth out of wearing, because anything else might have made him more likeable to her. And she didn't want to like him.

'We were talking about Danny,' she said, remembering why he had come.

'*You* were talking about Daniele,' he answered pointedly.

'Did you see him?' It suddenly occurred to her that he'd probably met his nephew if he'd been to the house first. 'Emiliano…' She ran after him as he strode purposefully back to the car.

'Not the time, nor the place,' he said dismissively as he skirted the vehicle and proceeded to open the front passenger door. 'I am wet and I am muddy and you look as if another five minutes out in this…' he tossed a glance towards the rain-hung trees and the heavier rain clouds that were gathering thickly across the valley '…will have you in bed with pneumonia.'

'I'm used to it,' Lauren told him, trying to sound nonchalant because the way his eyes were travelling over her drenched hair and her damp sweater and jeans was causing little flames of desire to lick along her veins, making her aware, for the first time since he'd arrived on the scene, of what an untidy mess she must look.

'Used to what?' he queried with a mocking twist to his mouth, holding open the car door. 'Being in bed with pneumonia? Or running round the countryside rescuing stray dogs?'

'Brutus isn't a stray. He's Stephen's dog,' she said with deliberate casualness and, from the formidable look she earned herself as she stepped into the car, gleaned a guilty satisfaction from knowing that her drenched hair was probably dripping all over his immaculate creamy leather upholstery.

Boiling a kettle of water in the farmhouse kitchen, Emiliano heard the pipework juddering from the flow of water in an upstairs bathroom.

'Go and shower,' he'd insisted as soon as she had let them in and, although she had resisted at first, she had seemed quite relieved to give in.

He couldn't get over how he had found her, out in these unpleasant conditions, trying to free that dog. Any more than he could get over how a cunning, gold-digging little siren of her calibre fitted into a run-down, home-spun environment like this.

Well, he would make her coffee and then he would tell her of his proposition. And if she didn't like him being fully involved in his nephew's life…then tough! She had had him to herself long enough. Now it was time for Daniele Cannavaro to know his father's family and to grow up fully aware of just who he was and exactly where he came from, even if Lauren Westwood didn't agree. There was no way he was going to relinquish responsibility for the boy, or abandon him, as his father had done. Nor would he ever allow him to feel pushed aside—as he himself had been.

Staring out of the multi-paned window at the wet and murky stable yard, he was so deep in thought that he hadn't realised that the water had stopped flowing in the pipes.

Suddenly a sound behind him had him swinging round, and the sight that met him stalled the breath in his lungs.

Lauren was coming through the doorway in a short silk floral robe that showed off every movement of her body—whether intentionally or otherwise—and her rough-towelled red hair, now left to dry naturally, was falling wildly about her shoulders. But every inch of her, right down to those long, slender feet with their clear varnished nails, was making Emiliano's mouth go dry and, in spite of all the terrible things he had been thinking about her, a shaft of hot desire was suddenly scorching through him.

He was leaning back against the sink with a mug of coffee in his hand, looking every bit at home in her lowly kitchen as he'd looked in the shameless luxury of that five-star hotel.

With his jacket discarded and his hair as wild and rumpled as his mud-stained shirt, he looked so untamed and spectacular that Lauren's heart-rate pumped up a level.

'Don't stand on ceremony. Help yourself to a biscuit.' The transparent jar in which she kept them beside the kettle had been pulled forward and its lid was on the counter, evidence that he had clearly helped himself already.

'You will have to excuse my manners,' he said, by way of an apology. 'I am afraid I haven't eaten for a few hours.'

She glanced at the jar, which was missing the last two of Danny's chocolate bourbons, leaving only the handful of plainer ones that she preferred. She wouldn't have minded, but she couldn't afford to replace them until she could cash her wages the day after tomorrow.

And you *accused* me *of trying to take from you.*

She didn't say it but the green eyes clashing with midnight-black expressed that exact sentiment as she crossed to one of the wall cupboards and took out a large round tin.

'I'm sorry it's only plain Madeira,' she said cynically as she was cutting a large chunk of the homemade cake on the kitchen table, 'but I didn't know you were coming. If I had, I would have definitely put something in it.'

'Then perhaps it is lucky for me that you didn't,' he drawled with the barest trace of a smile, leaving her in no doubt as to his meaning.

'Contrary to what you think about me, I don't go round trying to poison Italian billionaires,' she informed him bluntly. 'Not until I've married them and got them to change their last will and testament in my favour.'

He laughed, yet that harsh edge to the sound was unmistakable. 'Is that what you had in mind when you seduced me, *cara*?' His dark eyes were hooded, but there was softness now in that false endearment that made Lauren's legs feel as spongy as the cake she had just been slicing.

'Of course not!' Hot colour crept up her throat above the deep 'V' of her robe as she suddenly realised what she had as good as admitted to. And then, in an attempt to brush over it, she went on, with an involuntary glance over those superbly masculine shoulders, 'You would have been far too young and healthy for me to convince the world you died of natural causes.'

He laughed again, the sound more natural this time. 'Is that why you prefer older men like that smitten banker I saw you making eyes at at that party?'

'I wasn't making eyes at him! If you must know, he was boring me senseless!' She dumped the plate with the chunk of cake down on the counter in front of him. 'If you want anything else then the local pub does a cheap steak dinner on Fridays. I would cook you one myself but, as you've probably already discovered, I'm all out of savouries at the moment!' Ridiculously, she felt near to tears as she demanded, 'So what is it you want, besides food?'

'You know what I want,' he said.

He meant Danny. As if she could forget!

Meeting the disturbing clarity of his eyes, however, as he sank those strong white teeth into her cake, she wondered whether he was referring to something else altogether. Or was that just her mind working overtime because of the way he was making her feel?

He'd been wearing a tie earlier but must have slipped it into his pocket, because now the top buttons of his shirt were unfastened, exposing the corded strength of his throat.

Dry-mouthed, Lauren felt a little frisson run through her as her gaze came to rest on the dark shadow of hair spanning his chest through the fine material of his shirt.

She reached for the mug she hadn't realised he had filled while she had been cutting him some cake and the normality of the situation suddenly seemed laughable in the circumstances.

'What are you smiling about?'

Of course. He didn't miss a thing.

'Maybe it's because I'm being waited on in my own kitchen by a man who not only thinks I'm a gold-digger of the highest order, but a child abductor as well. That's got to be pretty amusing, don't you think?'

'So convince me you aren't.'

'I don't need to convince anyone of anything,' she assured him, watching him demolish his piece of Madeira cake in two bites.

He dipped his head in an oddly courtly gesture before putting his empty plate back on the worktop. Was he giving her the benefit of the doubt?

Sipping her coffee, she watched him rake one side of his hair back in that way that was such an integral part of him and which was already so familiar to her. It was then that she noticed the blood staining his shirt cuff, and the angry red marks above his hand on the underside of his right wrist.

'You cut yourself.' He must have done so out there when he had been trying to free Brutus earlier. Yet he hadn't given any indication of it. Not a murmur…

'It is nothing,' he dismissed, reaching round and picking up his own mug.

'Nothing?' Even from where she was standing, Lauren could see how inflamed and sore it looked. 'You'd better bathe that. Put some antiseptic on it or something. You can't just leave it.'

'Why not?' Draining his mug of its contents, he returned it to the kitchen counter.

'You could get tetanus or some other infection, especially where animals have been involved,' she told him, although he looked so fit and hard that she couldn't imagine any self-respecting bacteria attacking *him.* 'I really must advise you to get it cleaned up,' she pressed when she could see he had no intention of bothering.

'Why don't you do it for me?' he suggested in a way she hadn't heard him speak to her since that morning when she'd woken up, deliciously tender from his love-making and hungry for more, in his monstrous bed in that hotel room.

Her first instinct, though, was to tell him to go to hell. After all, he had treated her abominably when he'd misjudged her so completely after that wild night and morning when nothing but their need for each other had seemed to matter. That night and morning that had been the most amazing—and then the most humiliating—of her life!

She wasn't prepared to stoop to his level, however, deciding he wouldn't have cut himself so viciously if it hadn't been for her. And he *had* helped her with the dog.

Discarding her mug and grabbing some cotton wool from the first aid box she took out of the cupboard under the dresser, she went over to the sink and moistened it under the warm tap. Then, with her heart thumping ridiculously, she waited for him to unfasten a button and turn back his cuff before applying the cotton wool gingerly to his wound.

She heard his breath catch and felt him stiffen on that initial contact with his wrist.

'I'm sorry. I didn't mean to hurt you,' she expressed, as she would have done with anyone.

'Didn't you?' he responded dryly.

After that he stood without complaint as Lauren attended to his wound, catching his hand in her palm and carefully bathing away the grime from the painfully torn flesh.

With no words breaking the silence and only the

clock on the dresser ticking away the minutes, Lauren was painfully aware of Emiliano's regular breathing and the way he inhaled more deeply occasionally, as though he were breathing in the scented freshness of her hair.

And he wasn't the only one whose nostrils were working overtime! she thought as the familiar fragrance of his cologne made her head swim from the memories it evoked. The slight salty taste of his skin as her tongue had traced a provocative pattern over his contoured, hair-sprinkled chest. The way he had laughingly caught the hair at the nape of her neck to hold her there, governing her kisses along the exquisite symmetry of his strong, hard, masculine body.

Unable to stand there performing such a personal task for him while her mind was running riot with erotic images, she knew she had to say something. Huskily, she told him, 'I didn't plan what happened in London, you know. Even though you want to think I did.'

'Oh, I didn't want to, Lauren.' That deep chest expanded and fell again. 'It is, however, in the past and as such, it is best forgotten.'

'No, it isn't.' She'd be darned, she thought, if she let him—or anyone, for that matter—carry on thinking such a terrible thing about her. 'It might be something you can leave. But no one accuses me of something so nasty and gets away with it. I don't know what you think you heard when you were eavesdropping outside that room—and I know some of the things Vikki said left a lot to be desired. But whatever it was you heard or didn't hear *me* say really isn't my problem. And, whatever you think of me, I can tell you this much,

Emiliano Cannavaro. I wouldn't touch your money or your lifestyle with a bargepole! If you really think I'm holding on to Danny just for what monetary reward I can get out of it, then I'll tell you now that if you keep up that line of accusation it'll be me taking *you* to court for defamation of character!'

'Why don't you try using the scrubbing brush?' he suggested, with a wry glance down at his wrist, shaming her into realising just how fiercely she was rubbing at his skin.

'Perhaps I should have,' she responded, when she knew she should really have been apologising.

Instead, taking control of herself, she turned his dark wrist to inspect the wound and satisfy herself that it was completely clean. 'You really should put a plaster on that,' she advised, suddenly self-conscious of his proximity. And let out a gasp as he caught her wrist now, drawing her just a little too close for comfort.

'And you, *mia bella*, really should have put on more clothes.'

Lauren's mind screamed in rejection of the wild sensations that were suddenly leaping through her. 'Let me go!'

He laughed very softly. 'Not until we can come to some agreement about Daniele.'

Lauren tensed, trying to stifle the feelings that were coursing through her from his dangerous nearness, from the heady musk of him mingling with that subtle spice and from the thrilling latent strength lurking beneath the sophisticated, civilised exterior.

'You had my answer over the phone a few days ago. Now let me go!'

'When your pulse is throbbing beneath my fingers

like an Apache drumbeat? And your eyes, *cara mia*...
Those lovely eyes that spoke volumes to mine that
night they clashed across that ballroom are betraying you with their sultriness and telling me that bio-
logically we were meant to be lovers, no matter how
much we would both like to deny it and wish that it
could be different.'

She could have moved, Lauren thought. She could
have pulled back from him and he would have let her.
But his eyes and his voice were working on her senses
like some hypnotic drug, so that she felt paralysed
with wanting as his long fingers tugged gently at the
belt of her robe.

The silky fabric gave and fell away, leaving her
parted robe revealing minuscule purple briefs and the
full inner curves of her heavy breasts above her tiny
waist.

'You should have known better than to test my resistance, *cara*.' His voice was like a caressing purr coming from deep in his chest. 'Or your own.'

She hadn't wanted it to happen. But, as his arm
slipped around her waist and his mouth came down
over hers, she was pressing her nakedness against his
fully clothed body with every last drop of her raging need.

She hated the man! Why then was she letting him
do this to her? she tried reasoning wildly.

The rasp of his jaw against hers was an exciting demand, like the burning heat of him through the fine
silk shirt and the hard excitement of his strong and
hardening body.

All she knew was that she wanted this! Wanted *him!*

Here and now! No matter how much more shame and degradation would follow after.

When he pushed back her robe and his hand palmed the hard tip of one begging breast she could do nothing but arch into his mind-blowing caress.

'You are so beautiful,' he said thickly, with his teeth softly grazing her ear, then moving down the soft line of her jaw to her responsive neck and the sensitised juncture of her shoulder. But when he tilted her back against his arm and took the crest of her other breast into his mouth, Lauren gave a shuddering gasp of pure pleasure.

'I hate you.' It was an agonised little sound, but it was so important that he should know that.

He stopped suckling, turning his head against the upper swell of her breast. 'And that makes this perfectly acceptable?'

Did it?

No, it doesn't! her mind shrieked at her. *It's self-gratifying! Totally insane! And immoral!*

Her voice, croaky and shaking, didn't sound like hers at all, as somehow she managed to say, 'Nothing I do with you could ever be acceptable.'

'And it is that that makes it so exciting, is it not, *mia bella*? The fact that we both want this against our better judgement.'

'I—don't—want—you.' She could scarcely get the statement past her lips as each word came out punctuated with the effort it took.

Remarkably, Emiliano stood up and drew back.

'No,' he agreed, but the husky sound was tinged with mockery.

From his drawn-down lashes Lauren knew he was

noting the rosy swollen aureoles of her breasts, and quickly she pulled her robe together, belting it tightly. His face, though, was flushed, she noticed, and she didn't even need to look at him to know how hard he was. She had felt his arousal when he had ground his hips against hers and the thought of how she was responsible for that produced an almost excruciating ache between her thighs.

'OK, so I'm human. But don't feel so smug. You're rich and you're powerful and you aren't too bad-looking either. Isn't that an irresistible combination for any woman? As you said in London, being ensnared by someone doesn't mean you have to like them. And a woman can take as much as a man without it being expected to mean anything beyond the purely physical these days.'

A twisted sort of smile touched his mouth. It was clear that he was having as much of a battle as she was to bring his emotions back under control again.

'How very modern of you,' he breathed. 'In which case, you should find my proposition more appealing than I had imagined.'

Shakily she queried, 'What proposition?' She didn't know what he had in mind, but she was certain that she wasn't going to like it.

'Simply this,' he stated. 'That you allow me to take Daniele away for a month, but with a new condition.'

'Which is?'

'That you accompany him.'

He had to be joking!

'For what reason?' she prompted, her green eyes narrowing.

'He knows you.' His tone was clipped. 'He will be happier if you are around.'

Lauren looked at him cagily. 'And what do you get out of it?'

The mere lifting of one masculine eyebrow sent Lauren's pulses sky-high.

'Oh, don't look so affronted, Lauren,' he said. 'We could so easily have been having a totally different kind of…intercourse…' he glanced towards the ceiling '…up there if we had not called a halt to what we were doing just now. But it is clear we both still want what we indulged in two years ago, even though—as you say—we do not like each other. And to combine it with my getting to know Daniele—and vice versa— seems to me to be the perfect solution.'

It would, Lauren thought, the idea of what he was proposing sending sensual shivers along her spine. Yet how could she want him so much physically, she wondered, when he still continued to despise her? Because, in spite of what she had said, she didn't really believe that a woman could give her body so completely to a man without somehow getting herself emotionally involved with that man. She couldn't, anyway.

'And if I still won't agree?' She couldn't believe how much her voice was shaking. 'To let you take Danny, I mean. Either with or without *me*.'

'You know very well what the answer is to that,' he said in a voice that was brutally calm. 'Don't put me to the test, Lauren.'

The test being that he would fight her for him. That was what he was saying. A fight she was more than just a little afraid she would lose.

'I do not want to hurt you,' he said softly. 'But you will give me no choice if you refuse.'

'So you're giving me no choice instead?' Bitterness tinged her voice as she struggled with his ultimatum.

Another movement of an eyebrow said it all.

As she'd already pointed out, he was rich and powerful. He could tear her heart out if he wanted to. And he probably wanted to! she thought bitterly. Instead, he was offering her ecstasy. Physical ecstasy in return for not taking Danny away from her. Unbelievable physical ecstasy. And a suitcaseful of self-degradation when it was all over.

'All right. I'll accompany my nephew,' she told him with her voice cracking. 'To look after him and make sure that where he goes and what he does is in his best interest. But if you think that you and I will be picking up from where we left off two years ago, then you've got another think coming! I won't be your plaything, Emiliano. Not now or at any time in the future.'

Which was a ludicrous thing to say, she realised, in the circumstances. Because, as he'd already said, if things had taken their natural course just now, they would have been up there, lying on her single bed, with her allowing him to do all sorts of intimate things with her. Her only redemption lay in the fact that he didn't point that out to her for a second time.

'I'll be in touch in a day or two,' was all he said, before grabbing his jacket off the back of one of her second-hand chairs and informing her that he would see himself out.

It was only after the front door had closed behind him and she was listening for the growl of the powerful car that Lauren realised she had been so disconcerted by his proposition and by agreeing to accompany him that she hadn't even thought to ask where they were going.

CHAPTER FOUR

LOUNGING ON THE canopied terrace of his Caribbean retreat, looking out across the crescent of pink sand to the young woman and toddler paddling at the water's edge, Emiliano couldn't believe his luck.

He hadn't expected Lauren to give in quite so easily when he had insisted that she accompany him here with Daniele—or Danny, as she insisted on calling him. But then, as she had pointed out so bluntly when he had first told her what he was proposing, he hadn't really given her any choice. If he had, there was no doubt in his mind that she wouldn't be down there on that beach right now. And after that moment when he had slipped the belt of her robe and he'd realised how much he could still affect her—how much she still affected him—it had suddenly become imperative that she should come.

His hooded eyes moved from the toddler standing with his arm outstretched, to the beautiful redhead in the pale blue bikini, which concealed very little of her perfect hourglass figure.

Her flaming hair was piled up in a way that emphasised her slender neck and back; her skin was already softly tanned because of the time she spent outdoors.

He saw her bend down to the little boy and take whatever it was—probably a shell—he was offering her. Then she said something laughingly to him as she gently pushed his wind-blown hair back off his face.

They both wanted Daniele, Emiliano thought. But they couldn't both have him—not without it being detrimental to the child's wellbeing—and he could see Lauren and himself reaching a kind of impasse over it.

When he had gone to see her that first time over two weeks ago, he had thought it would be easy—that she would hand over his nephew with no questions asked if the price was right. What he hadn't expected to find was a natural-living girl with a fierce set of values, far removed from the vamp he thought he had taken to bed in London, which had made him start to wonder whether he hadn't been too hasty in judging her.

Her laughter drifted up to him with the toddler's giggles as she pretended to chase him over the carpet of pink sand. Suddenly she swooped down and picked him up, and he squealed with delight, his dark head nuzzling into her throat, one tiny hand laid innocently against a breast that was almost spilling out of its cup from the energetic game they had been playing. Then she swung back to point out a speedboat on the glittering blue water and the sight of those lovely buttocks— bare, save for the tantalising blue string that separated them—had his throbbing anatomy sending him a loud and clear message. He needed to have her alone!

Minutes later she was chasing the squealing toddler over the beach again, but made a grab for him as they reached the steps to the pool terrace, climbing them with the child in her arms.

Between two huge pots of hibiscus flowers and a powdery scented oleander bush that was growing near the stone balustrade at the top of the steps, she put him down so that he could run to Emiliano.

'*Buongiorno, piccolo.*' It was the first time he had spoken to his nephew this morning, who was clinging to his cut-off jeans, grinning up at him with his baby-toothed smile.

Leaning forward, Emiliano snaked an arm around him and then, with both arms, lifted him laughingly into the air. 'Has your aunt been making you run all the way up the beach?' he asked the giggling Daniele. He turned an ear to the child's face. 'She has? *Buon cielo!* Shall I spank her or will you?'

'Perhaps *she* doesn't want to be spanked,' Lauren contested, but there was a quiver in her voice, he noted, with that unmistakable flush colouring her cheeks.

'Since when did punishment ever have anything to do with what one wants?' he put to her with sensual teasing in his eyes.

'Is that why you brought me here, Emiliano?' she asked levelly, though he could sense the tension in her slender body. 'To punish me?'

'If it is,' he murmured, 'then it is I who is being punished.'

She frowned before her gaze fell—involuntarily he felt—to the khaki fabric that was pulling across his lap.

'Good,' she exhaled, understanding, and yet he detected a slight tremor in her voice again and that tension that made her nostrils dilate as she stood, unaware of how provocative she looked, with her slender hands splayed against the gentle curve of her hips and her lovely breasts straining against the bikini.

Or perhaps she was, he thought.

If they had been on their own he would have pulled her down across his lap right there and then and enjoyed her shriek of surprise, and almost certainly excitement too, he decided, at anticipating what he would never have dreamed of actually carrying out. But had he been the old-fashioned type of chauvinist, he fantasised—which he certainly wasn't and never had been—at least it would have got her into his arms...

Knowing he shouldn't be entertaining such inappropriate thoughts, especially in Daniele's company, he set the little boy gently down on his feet again.

A subtle lifting of his hand brought his Afro-Caribbean housekeeper, who had just finished discussing something with one of the groundsmen and was about to go into the house, over to their little gathering.

'Constance, would you kindly take this little man here away for his well-deserved nap?' He looked indulgently down at the child, palming his soft baby cheek. '*Grazie*,' he said, the word sliding off his tongue like molten honey.

The appreciative smile he gave the woman as she swung the toddler up into her generously proportioned arms could have melted her where she stood, Lauren reluctantly decided, if Constance Dowden—as she had been introduced to Lauren the day before—hadn't been a generation above him.

'I haven't seen nearly enough of him,' Emiliano said, sounding regretful as the boy and the woman disappeared into the air-conditioned comfort of his tropical home.

A white, exclusively designed house, with intri-

cately wrought balconies and bougainvillaea-draped
walls, it stood in its own grounds against the lush green
vegetation that clothed the hillsides right down to its
private palm-fringed beach that was only accessible
from the house and the sea. The understated elegance
and simplicity of its interior had surprised Lauren
when they had arrived here yesterday, coming by private jet from Heathrow to one of the larger islands and
then by private launch to this less populated island
paradise. She'd imagined Emiliano favouring the more
glitzy, celebrity-decked resorts that his brother had.

'No, you haven't,' she agreed, bristling from the way
Danny had been effectively whisked away from her as
she sank down on the deep floral cushion of the cane
chair opposite Emiliano and picked up the tall glass
of iced tea from the table beside it that someone had
poured for her earlier.

Emiliano directed a hard and questioning glance at her.
Was that disapproval in her voice? he wondered. Or
was that just his conscience telling him that he should
have pressed his brother harder to have informed him
of Danny's whereabouts, instead of allowing himself
to be brushed off with lame answers?

'I know I sent him gifts, but that was not enough.'

'You did?' Lauren's words were strung with surprise as she sipped her tea. 'We didn't receive any
gifts.' From the way her forehead pleated he could
tell they had never reached his nephew. 'What sort
of gifts?'

'Oh…' He shook his head, lips pursing as he plundered his memory banks. 'I don't know…Some sort of
baby tractor for him to ride on. A bear…'

She was looking at him as though she couldn't imagine him doing anything so trivial as picking out gifts for a baby.

'I gave them to Angelo. He said he would give them to him.'

'He didn't.'

Emiliano's dark brows came together. No maintenance for Daniele. A recent scour through the mess of Angelo's financial records had shown that no payments at all had been made or even claimed for the little boy. Not even a gift passed on from his only uncle. He couldn't comprehend what his brother had been thinking of.

'Why didn't you tell me Angelo was not providing you with any money for Danny?' he asked, appalled. 'Why did you not try to claim?'

'Because he didn't want anything to do with his son,' she said, putting her glass back down. 'I did invite him to see him sometimes, but he never came. So I decided that if he didn't want anything to do with us, then we wouldn't have anything to do with him. Or any of you,' she tagged on after a moment, as though it had taken a little extra courage to say it.

In other words, she was too grossly independent to ask anyone for anything. He was beginning to see that now. He was also being forced to accept that he had judged her far too readily two years ago when he had bracketed her as the same type of opportunist female as her sister. She was nothing like Vikki Westwood, whose character he had sussed right from the moment Angelo had introduced her to him outside that Rome restaurant where they had met for dinner.

He remembered welcoming her to the family when

his brother had said that they were getting engaged; remembered how she had laughed flirtatiously, turning her head so that the brotherly kiss he'd intended for her cheek had landed on her full red lips. He'd known then that Vikki Westwood was going to be trouble.

'Does this mean you believe me now?'

'What it means, Lauren, is that I don't understand how you could have let my brother get away with it. And I repeat…Why didn't you come to me?'

Above the sighing of the warm wind through the oleander bush he heard an incredulous little sound leave her throat, and knew the answer even before she replied.

'After you'd accused me of sleeping with you because you thought I was after your money? I'm not a glutton for humiliation, Emiliano. And your wonderful brother would have denied it anyway.'

'I don't think so,' he countered. And when she looked at him as though he were suddenly challenging the truthfulness of all she had been saying, 'He would have told me simply to mind my own business,' he clarified. Wasn't that what Angelo had always said to him when he had quizzed his brother about anything that he wasn't comfortable with? Not pulling his weight in the company. His drinking habits. The way he treated women. Daniele.

Wondering at the emotion that seemed to darken those heart-stopping features, Lauren had to force back a sudden dangerous surge of warm feeling towards him.

Instead, in response to that remark he had made about his brother telling him to mind his own business, she suggested a little shakily, 'Perhaps I should take that stance with you myself.'

'Oh?' He looked at her obliquely, the sunlight creeping under the canopy glinting on the rich, healthy sheen of his hair.

'Just because I've agreed to come here with you doesn't mean I've agreed to let anyone else take over looking after Danny,' she told him, with her gaze automatically straying to where the other woman had taken her nephew.

'And you think that anything to do with Daniele isn't my business too?'

He had a point, but right at that moment Lauren had been left feeling too dispensable over not being consulted.

'He's still in my care and OK…I'll let Constance do it this once as she was kind enough to agree to. But in future I intend to bathe and feed him and tuck him up in bed as I've always done.'

'And so you shall, if that is what you want,' he acceded, surprising her. 'I merely thought that, for the time being, you might appreciate a break.'

She did, now that he mentioned it. It was just that she felt so protective and possessive of her nephew where Angelo's older brother was concerned that she realised she'd been guilty of a gross case of overreacting.

'It's important even for a full-time aunt to relax sometimes,' he said. 'Something which I think you have done very little of over the past year, am I not right?'

'You are,' Lauren murmured and, after a moment, in an attempt to redeem herself for her churlish behaviour, tagged on rather sheepishly, 'Thanks.'

'In that case…' He was tugging off his T-shirt and tossing it aside, exposing broad bronzed shoulders and that hair-dusted, beautifully contoured chest. 'You and I are going to have some fun. Come on!'

Before she had time to gather her wits, he had grabbed her hand and was pulling her up from her chair, and she could only run after him down the steps, trying to match his pace as he urged her onwards over the sand.

'Hey! Hang on!' she gasped, breathless more from his actions than from trying to keep up with him. 'I'm afraid I can't run anywhere near as fast as you!'

'Of course not. How silly of me,' he said, stopping so suddenly that she found herself careering into him.

Swiftly, her hands shot up to steady her, and she sucked in a breath as her fingers met the warm hard musculature of his chest.

'Touching me, Lauren?' His voice and his smile mocked. 'I thought that was against the rules.'

'Are there any rules?' Against the sound of the waves breaking over the damp sand, her voice quavered. 'Other than the ones that you make?'

He didn't respond, only to click his tongue in laughing disapproval, the sound closer, so close she could feel his warm breath fanning her hair.

'And if there were, you'd break them,' she accused.

As he broke people. Across the years, her younger sister's words drifted back to her. As he would probably break *her*—and anyone who didn't submit to his will.

'Are you afraid of me?'

To Lauren, it was like some sort of déjà vu. Hadn't

he said something along those lines that very same
night at that party?

'No.' She said it too quickly because she was. Or
at least, she thought, afraid of the pain he could cause
her if he asserted his claim over his nephew. But it
was herself she was afraid of right at that moment. Of
her responses to his nearness and his physicality that
were making her blood surge like the waves and her
heart pulse with an excitement that was totally erotic.

'*Santo cielo!*' It was a swift, sharp utterance under
his breath. 'I think right now, *mia bella,* we both need
cooling off.'

She was being lifted off her feet, and so unexpectedly that she let out a surprised shriek as she found
herself caught against the surging strength of his hard,
virile body.

'Put me down!'

'I thought you said there are no rules.'

'There are,' she stressed, suddenly panicky.

'Well, just as you said, I am breaking them.' He
was wading with her into the translucent aquamarine
water, which was coming further up his muscular legs
with every powerful stride he took.

'What are you going to do?' She didn't know and
she wasn't looking forward to finding out. 'Please don't
throw me in.'

'I would not dream of it.' He grinned.

'*Please!*' She swivelled her head towards the water
and back to his strong teasing features. 'You'll be sorry
if you do!'

'Such spirit!' He laughed. 'And what could you do
to me, *mia cara,* that would make my regret really not
worth dropping you?'

'You dare!' He was laughing and it was exciting her. Nevertheless, she tightened her hold around his neck and superbly masculine shoulder, clinging to him for all she was worth.

'What is the matter?' he asked. 'Can you not swim?'

'Not this far out. I'll panic. *Please!*'

He was still laughing. 'And there I was imagining you were a woman who could do anything.'

'I am.' She was adamant about that. 'But my survival tactics don't extend to being thrown into the sea.' Only to big hunky Italians who threatened mischief just to get a woman to cling to them, she thought, suddenly aware of exactly what game he was playing.

'OK. So drop me! Come on, you big bully. Let me see…ahhh!'

The splash as she hit the water was nonetheless an unexpected shock. But quickly, as the water closed over her, she was already recovering herself.

Swiftly, she struck out and down and, seeing those strong feet planted firmly on the sea bed, she reached out and grabbed one muscular leg, toppling him off-balance as she took him totally unawares.

She was back on her feet and wading towards the shore when she heard the thrust of his body breaking through the water.

'So you can't swim, huh?' There was the promise of some exciting retribution in his voice as he stood up and starting wading in pursuit, and it suddenly dawned on Lauren that he must have seen her slicing through the pool that morning before anyone was up. He would never have thrown her in like that otherwise. 'You had better stand there and wait for me, *cara*, because you are not going to get away!'

Was he kidding?

Reaching the shore, she raced off along the beach towards the inviting shade of the palm trees, the wet sand like warmed cream beneath her feet.

He had gained on her even before she could change her mind and dart off towards the house and suddenly she felt too scantily clothed to be playing this game with him.

'You're all wet,' she breathed, laughing as she turned around. She was running backwards, taking in the rivulets streaming down his face and the hair that was plastered to his skull. Her body was pulsing with a reckless excitement as she noted the determination stamped on every pursuing inch of him.

'I wonder why!'

'You deserved it.'

He was laughing, but his eyes held a dark intent. 'You really think so?'

'OK. I'm sorry!'

'Too late.' He'd slowed his pace, but still kept coming.

'It's never too late.' She put up her hands as he moved like a slow, stealthy predator over the sand. 'You'll be sorry,' she promised, battling with the rising excitement coursing through her.

'I think not,' he said in a voice that was softly mocking. 'And I think, *mia cara*, that we have definitely been there before.'

Just a few minutes ago, she thought chaotically, and gasped as her heel caught on a small, smooth stone between the trees and she landed flat on her back.

His soft laughter was a sensuous excitement on her racing senses.

'OK.' With the strands of her wet hair twisting over one shoulder, she raised herself up on her elbows to say challengingly, 'So what are you proposing to do now?'

His dark hooded eyes slid to the rapid rise and fall of her breasts, which were accentuated by the provocative pose.

'Something you have been wanting me to do from the moment you saw me walking across that stable yard. Something we were never able to leave alone from the moment we saw each other at that farce of a pre-nuptial party.'

Standing above her now, he suddenly stooped and started to lower himself towards her, the veins in his powerful arms standing out as they supported his weight at full stretch, so that miraculously he wasn't actually touching her.

Just the promise of all that masculine strength pressing down on her made her head swim with dizzying desire. She fell back on the sand to widen the space between them, and yet inviting the whole exciting length of his hard wet body.

She let out a shuddering gasp as he brought it down over her softness, her words trembling as she uttered, 'You're a bastard.'

'And you like it.'

Dear heaven! Did she? Was she so sick that she could only find pleasure and arousal in drawing swords, as he'd once described it, with a man who despised her and who hadn't spared a single feeling for letting her know it?

'No, I don't.' Her breathing was becoming more ragged by the second, giving the lie to her statement.

'But you like this.' It was a whispered caress against

her throat, making her whimper from the delicious sensation. 'And this.' His teeth grazed the underside of her jaw, moving upwards along the soft curve of her cheek. 'And if I remember the language of your body from those hours that you graced my bed, *carissima*, it positively pleaded with me to do this.'

Just the action of her bikini top being pulled down dragged a guttural sound from her throat and made her body sing in wild anticipation.

'Open your eyes.'

Reluctantly, her eyelids fluttered apart.

Her breasts were heavy and swollen, spread out like a feast before him, and now he watched the way her eyes darkened and her face crumpled in agonising pleasure as his hands caressed their hardened, sensitive crests.

Desire sent a burning arrow of need piercing through her to the heart of her femininity.

It was Nature's way, she thought through a spiral of heightening yet dismaying pleasure, that this man who didn't even like her could turn her on as easily as if he were flicking switches, and trigger electrical impulses that opened up other circuits of her body to his will.

'Emiliano…' His name felt like music on her lips.

He lowered his head and covered her mouth with his and she responded to it with a deep groan of satisfaction, her mouth widening to allow the kiss to deepen, her fingers clutching at his strong wet hair, her breath mingling, tongue blending with his.

He was warm and wet and strong, his weight an erotic pleasure pressing her into the sand.

His body hair rasped against her breasts and against the comparative smoothness of her parting thighs. His arousal nudged her through the wet triangle of her bikini bottom, making her wriggle beneath him and thrust her pelvis upwards for the greater intimacy she craved.

She was his—and he knew it. A slave to her eternal need for this man that she'd thought had died. Killed off by his flaying remarks at that wedding and the shame and humiliation she had had to deal with afterwards. But it hadn't been. And now, as his hands reclaimed her luscious breasts, pushing them up to take each throbbing crest in his mouth in turn, she writhed beneath him like a wild nymph, debauched, untamed and wholly abandoned.

'Your body was made for loving.' Emiliano's voice was hoarse with desire. 'But not by just anyone.' He drew her breast more deeply into his mouth before letting it go. 'Loving by me. We both recognised that as soon as we kissed that first time, did we not, *mia bella*?'

Groaning her agreement, Lauren arched her back, unable to get enough of his exquisite torture.

She was his plaything, she realised. Nothing more. And it was going against everything she had said and believed in as an independent, free-thinking woman. But right now her body was in control of her and it wanted nothing more than to have this one man lie with her—play with her—and, having admitted that, she lifted her arms above her head in an arc of total submission.

Acknowledging it, he slipped his hands under her taut buttocks and pulled her lower body hard against the thrilling evidence of his need.

He was hot and hard—as hard as she was soft—and

she was more than ready for him. There was only the barrier of her string to be removed and she would be taking him into her. Only a few more seconds and...

She wasn't protected!

The thought rushed at her, dragging her sufficiently out of her sensual torpor to recognise something else. The sound of a child crying!

Danny!

She could hear him wailing from somewhere in the house, bawling away at the top of his little lungs.

'I've got to go!'

She was wriggling under Emiliano, but this time for her freedom. It took him only a second to realise why.

'I expect, like all little boys, he is objecting to being bathed,' he remarked, sounding less concerned than she was, reminding her that she had mentioned Danny's aversion to bath time to him on the plane the previous day.

'No. It's not that sort of cry.' She was already on her feet, quickly adjusting her bikini top. 'Something's wrong. I've got to go!'

Her body was aching with frustration. But none of that compared to the anguish that was gnawing at her as she raced, full pelt, across the sand.

She knew Emiliano would need a minute to compose himself before he followed her. Nevertheless, he had caught up with her by the time she reached the steps to the terrace.

Now they both looked up as Constance came running out through the front porch.

'Oh Mr Cannavaro, I was coming to look for you. The little boy—he's inconsolable. I tried to put him to bed but he keeps screaming for Miss Westwood.

I thought maybe he'd been stung, but I don't think that's what it is.'

Fraught with worry, Lauren raced through the luxurious house and straight up to the little room that only days ago, she'd been told, had been furnished as a nursery. A huge Norfolk Island Pine outside in the grounds shaded it from the heat of the afternoon sun.

A young maid was bouncing the screaming toddler on her hip, but the little boy was refusing to be pacified.

Red-faced, tears streaming down his cheeks, he wailed even louder when he saw Lauren enter the room and instantly held out his arms for her to pick him up.

'It's all right,' she breathed against his hot little face. 'It's all right, Danny. I'm here. Mummy's here.'

She didn't know why she'd said that. At her own decision he'd called her 'Laa-wen' from the moment he'd learned to talk. It was something she'd decided was right as she was simply his aunt and hadn't wanted to feel as though she was betraying Vikki. Pushing her sister aside. Taking her place.

But perhaps it was the sudden fierce protectiveness that had surged up in her as she had caught his convulsive little body to her that had made it come naturally to her to say it. Thankfully now, though, the screams had subsided, replaced by merely tearful sobbing over being abandoned.

'Has he been stung?'

She'd forgotten all about Emiliano.

Glancing up over the toddler's head, she noticed that his strong features were grooved with concern.

'No,' she assured him, relieved by the swift survey

she'd already made of the little face and limbs that there was nothing to worry about on that score.

'How can you be sure?' he quizzed, still looking anxious.

'He wouldn't have quietened down so quickly if he had been. He just isn't used to anyone else other than me and Fiona putting him to bed.'

Beneath the pale T-shirt Emiliano had obviously grabbed from the terrace on his way up here, his wide shoulders visibly relaxed. Shoulders that had felt like satin-clad steel beneath her hands...

With a jolt of something like shame, she realised that they might have been making full-blown love now if they hadn't been so fortuitously interrupted. With no protection, she reminded herself, remembering that Emiliano had never been so reckless before. She wondered if, when the moment had come, either of them would have had the strength of will to pull back.

Would Emiliano have thought of it? Or even asked her? she wondered. Or had he automatically assumed she was on the Pill?

She couldn't meet the dark intensity of his eyes as she rocked the infant, who was drifting off to sleep against her shoulder, sucking contentedly on his knuckles.

Was he thinking about what they'd been doing? Regretting the interruption? Or just relieved that she'd known what was wrong with his nephew?

Whichever, she decided, blanking her mind to what had happened out there. She could tell him something that fitted all probabilities, and said assuredly, 'That's what being a parent is all about.'

Suddenly his lashes came down and his dark Latin features became an inscrutable mask.

Perhaps he didn't like having to acknowledge how much Danny needed her, she thought, before he turned away, leaving her and Constance and the young maid to cope without him.

CHAPTER FIVE

OVER THE NEXT few days Lauren came to appreciate the meaning of the phrase 'tropical paradise' when every day was spent in utter relaxation.

There were barbecues on the beach, with Emiliano pointing out the pelicans to Daniele as they dived—sometimes three of them in unison—into the surging aquamarine waves for fish. Then there were times when Emiliano went out to attend to some local business and, with Daniele having his afternoon nap, Lauren was left alone to enjoy the peace of her surroundings, basking on a sunbed on the balcony beyond the luxuriously feminine bedroom they had given her, reading a book, or simply just lying back under the cool canopy of the terrace and listening to the eternal waves breaking on the deserted beach below the house.

The only thing that detracted from her total enjoyment of such a holiday of a lifetime was the mutual attraction between herself and Emiliano.

'I know you thought that in agreeing to come here I was consenting to us taking up where we left off two years ago, but I'm not,' she told him, sitting on a lounger and rubbing sunscreen into Daniele's delicate skin the morning after that shamefully intimate scene with Emiliano on the beach. 'It isn't going to help matters. In fact, it's only going to complicate things, so we're just going to have to curb any further developments on that score.'

All he had done was send her a dubious look and said only, 'Can we?' and with so much scepticism that even that had started her blood throbbing in her veins.

But he was right. How could they? Lauren thought. He only had to come within feet of her to make her body pulse with reckless excitement. Consequently, she felt tense and uneasy around him.

Like the morning she came down into the cooler atmosphere of the salon and found him, with his foot resting on the low sill of the open window, gazing out to sea as he talked formally to someone on the phone.

'I'm sorry.' Though they had been as intimate with each other in the past as it was possible to get, Lauren knew she had no real place, either in his private life or in his business affairs, and quickly made to withdraw.

Seeing her, he raised his hand in a detaining gesture, and hesitantly she moved back across the room.

'Thank you,' she heard him saying. 'I'd be honoured to speak at the opening ceremony. 'I look forward to it,' he expressed.

And with natural warmth, Lauren decided, guessing that he had just made some local official very happy.

'You're very popular with the people here,' she observed aloud as he came off the phone. 'Constance told me they've even named a ward after you at the hospital.' For funding a much needed and expensive piece of equipment, she remembered the housekeeper telling her proudly, which meant that the islanders didn't have to travel to one of the larger islands for the specialised treatment they might need.

'*Sì*,' he confirmed, turning to face her now, and then with a lack of pretentiousness that she was beginning to expect from him, added, 'but it was a joint enterprise. I did not do it alone. It took a great deal of hard work and awareness-raising by a lot of members of the community. All I did was present the final cheque.'

As if it was nothing! Lauren thought, having looked up his involvement with the hospital on the Internet and discovered how generous he had been. She was beginning to realise that there was far more depth to this complex man than she could ever have given him credit for.

'I thought you might like to look at these. Some time when you aren't too busy,' she added hastily, suddenly feeling awkward handing something so trivial as a baby album to a man who helped people cross continents and supplied hospitals with machines that made the difference between life and death.

He was looking at the gold lettering embossed on the cover. '"Our baby",' he read aloud, with a curious twist to his mouth.

'I bought it for Vikki and Angelo, but they'd split up before I could give it to them,' she said quickly, hoping he wasn't drawing any wrong conclusions from it—like imagining she was calling Danny theirs, as though he were a child they had created between them. 'Babies always have albums,' she went on. 'I didn't want Danny to miss out just because he didn't have a mother, and a father who didn't want to know him, so I put all the photos I took of him in there from when he was a tiny baby, plus the ones I've taken since he's been with me.'

He was turning over the pages, pausing now and then as one particular photograph caught his eye, and Lauren couldn't help noticing how good his hands looked against the soft white leather, the nails clean and cut straight across, the fingers long and tanned.

'You have kept a whole record.' He sounded impressed. 'I should be grateful to you.'

For when she handed Danny over?

Fear stabbed her in the chest, making her suddenly snap, 'Thanks. But I didn't do it for you.' Although she had—in part, she realised, just in case his father and the rest of the Cannavaro family ever realised what they were missing in abandoning their own flesh and blood. 'Well, Vikki and Angelo didn't bother,' she tagged on when she saw the way Emiliano's eyebrow had lifted at her change of tone and what had been, even to her own ears, a rather juvenile remark.

Looking as breathtaking in his casual clothes as he did when he was dressed for business, he was giving her all of his attention now.

'Why is it that whenever it comes round to the subject of my nephew you turn extremely defensive, Lauren?'

Her shoulders went back as she sucked in a deep breath. 'Perhaps it's because of references like that.'

'Like what?' His eyes narrowed as he studied her tight, tense features.

'*My* nephew,' she echoed with emphasis.

'But he *is* my nephew!' Incredulity coloured his voice. 'And I have made no secret of the fact that I'm hoping he will soon become my adopted son.'

'Over my dead body!'

'I hardly think,' he said, pulling a face, 'that I would really need to resort to such drastic action as that. Apart from which—' his mouth tugged wryly '—I prefer your body just the way it is.'

'It isn't funny!'

'No, it is not,' he agreed, suddenly turning serious. 'For heaven's sake, Lauren! Try to see the logic in this. Every boy needs a father.'

'No more than he needs a mother.'

'That's debatable.'

'Not to me, it isn't!'

'Can you not understand,' he said in more conciliatory tones, laying the album aside, 'that I just want the best for Daniele?'

'And you think I don't?'

'I know how much you care about him—'

'You couldn't possibly.'

'But would it not be fairer,' he suggested, ignoring her rejoinder, 'to allow him to have the start in life that you as a single parent, and in your position, could never provide?'

Was she being unfair?

Emotion bubbled up inside her from the mere suggestion that she might be. Was she being selfish denying Vikki's child the right to all his father's family could provide?

'*You'd* be a single parent,' she pointed out lamely. 'As well as a man.' But what a man! she thought grudgingly, unable to drag her gaze from his almost intimidating masculinity, as he stood, legs apart, towering above her in stature, status and that undeniable authority that could sway even the most prejudiced of minds in his favour.

'*Sì*, but with a whole entourage of advisers and nannies that I could easily afford to pay.'

'And you think advisers and nannies can give him the love he needs and stop him from waking up screaming in the night because he's been wrenched away from the only family he's ever known?' she argued as he moved closer to her. 'No!' As his hands came to rest on her shoulders she pulled forcefully away. 'You're not getting round me like that!'

Dear heaven! If he tried, she thought, it would make a mockery of everything she had said about not getting involved with him, because she knew she was too weak to resist him.

His arms fell to his sides, his shoulders dropping beneath the cream-coloured T-shirt he wore with light linen trousers. 'This is getting us nowhere,' he said heavily.

'No, it isn't,' she agreed.

'I don't want to fight with you, Lauren.' He sounded weary all of a sudden. 'Fighting is such an unproductive waste of time.'

'Then don't,' she advised him, suddenly near to tears, and swung away from him, out of the room, before he could guess at how defeated she felt.

Despite that, though, Emiliano was bonding surprisingly well with Danny, Lauren noted with mixed feelings over the next couple of weeks. Already Emiliano seemed to be laying plans for their nephew to become a champion swimmer, she thought and, in a lighter moment, told him so, while silently marvelling at how gentle and patient he was with the child who, with little floats attached to his tiny arms, was splashing around, squealing delightedly, while Emiliano held him in the garden's shaded pool.

In turn, in his own way, the toddler was instructing Emiliano as to what being a hands-on uncle was all about, and Lauren couldn't help but be amazed at how well Emiliano took to it. Like letting his nephew use him as a climbing frame while he was relaxing, either indoors or outside on one of the loungers, or like spreading his big body on the floor of the salon while helping him construct small towers out of the toy bricks he had bought for him, even though Daniele seemed to be much happier knocking them down.

The little boy was even letting Emiliano and Constance put him to bed these days whenever Lauren was willing to let them, but it was still his aunt he ran to on those occasions when he toppled over, too enthusiastic on his little legs; only Lauren who could provide the comfort he howled for as she rubbed his knees and kissed away his tears.

'I think you have earned a night out,' Emiliano told her one evening when she had finally got a very active Daniele off to sleep after what seemed like hours after she had put him to bed.

'I thought you were going to say a knighthood,' she whispered with a tired smile, glad that he had come looking for her in the nursery earlier and stayed to share the load, yet affected by him so unbearably that she felt drained of every last one of her emotional resources.

He grimaced. 'That too,' he said, obviously noticing how sleepy she looked. 'You go to bed. I will stay here for a while in case he wakes again.' And when she hesitated, 'Go on,' he insisted. 'But tomorrow night you will be coming out with me.'

The following evening he took her out to dine at a harbourside restaurant, where rum cocktails flowed like water and where Lauren was careful to resist a second after feeling the punch packed simply by one.

'That's better,' he said quietly from across the table, as the tensions she had been harbouring from just being around him over the past two weeks started to ebb away and her shoulders visibly relaxed.

He had finished his meal some time ago, and now, finishing hers, Lauren went to pick up her cell phone that was lying on the table.

'No,' Emiliano advised, reaching across and lightly covering her hand with his. 'He will be all right,' he emphasised in that same soft voice. 'Constance will call us if he isn't.' But he didn't withdraw his hand or that cool gaze from her face and, after a heart-stopping moment, he said, 'You know you really are remarkably beautiful.'

Lauren lifted her gaze to his magnificent bone structure and the breathtaking clarity of his eyes and, with a little quiver along her spine, answered, 'So are you.'

He laughed very softly, his voice carrying above the chink of glasses at the open-air bar and the exotic sounds from a steel band playing further along the wharf.

It had still been light when he had brought her here, driving around the coast on narrow winding roads, between sensational white beaches and thickly forested hillsides to uncover this amazing rendezvous.

A Colonial-style bar, perfectly circular in structure, its tree-shaded tables and chairs were scattered along the waterfront, where sailboats bobbed on their moorings alongside catamarans and fishing boats and, further out, beyond the stretching arm of the jetty, several luxury yachts graced the silent waters of the lagoon. Across the other side of the lagoon, rising into the hills, were private mansions, set like jaw-dropping gems above the coastline.

When they had first arrived she had seen their spectacular walled gardens awash with colour, from the paper-like flowers of bougainvillaea varying from red and purple to magenta, to the heavy pink clusters of oleander and the white and yellow stars of the sweet-scented frangipani.

Now it was dark and the very air was humming with the song of crickets and tiny lizards. Lights glowed from the yachts, one of which—a monster of a thing—had come in while they had been sitting there, while lanterns spilled light down from the almond trees, casting leafy shadows over the couples seated at other tables and over the strong features of the man sitting opposite her.

'If I owned a house here I'd never want to leave,' Lauren expressed tremulously, drawing her hand from under his, although she could still feel the burn of his touch as tangibly as the warm wind that caressed her bare shoulders and the humidity that was teasing her loose hair into tendrils around her face.

'Which is why I try to divide my time between my home in Italy and the one I have here,' he informed her, accepting her nervous rejection and sitting back on his chair, 'although I will probably be spending much more time in this part of the world from now on.'

He had told her two weeks ago that his company was taking over an ailing American cruise line and that being in the Caribbean meant that he could fly to the States and the hub of all the negotiations and activity and attend necessary meetings far more quickly than he could from Rome. A wry smile touched his mouth. 'Do I take it from your obvious appreciation that you are not sorry you came?'

How could she be? Lauren thought, although telling him that would be one sure step towards lessening her resistance to him. And so, with a secretive little smile that she couldn't have hidden even if she'd tried, she asked, changing the subject, 'Did you ever want to do anything else besides run the company? Or was it always a foregone conclusion that you would?'

'Always,' he responded succinctly. 'I was my father's heir.' His mouth compressed as though his thoughts had led him into some inner chamber of his mind to where Lauren definitely couldn't follow. 'Like your heir to the throne, I was schooled, educated and primed for that very purpose,' he continued, but there was an edge to his voice that hadn't been there a minute ago.

'And not Angelo?' Lauren asked, surprised.

'No.' His chest rose and fell steeply before he said, 'Angelo was allowed to follow whatever path he chose.'

Which was a path of self-destruction, Lauren thought unhappily. In the end.

From the stark emotion that made his cheekbones stand out in the arresting structure of his face, it was clear Emiliano was thinking along the same lines.

'And did you resent that?'

She wasn't sure why she asked it, and the flicker of danger she read in his eyes made her suddenly fear she had spoken out of turn.

She was surprised, therefore, when he exhaled deeply and answered, 'Yes. I resented it.'

'But you were happy as a child?' He wasn't saying so, but some surfacing memory led her to wonder whether he had been.

On the eve of their siblings' wedding he had given her scant insight into why he hadn't been Angelo's best man. His brother and he had moved on. Made their own lives, he'd said simply, which had seemed to explain why the role had fallen to the bridegroom's closest friend. Yet there had been strained feeling, Lauren had detected, between the two brothers, noticeable in the way Angelo had praised Emiliano with a kind of cynical self-mockery, as though he was jealous and resentful of his older brother in some way, and not the other way around. There had been a strained politeness too, she had sensed, between Emiliano and Claudette Cannavaro, the middle-aged, amazingly glamorous French ex-model who had been introduced to Lauren as the brothers' stepmother. Lauren remembered her as a rather distant, rock-hard beauty who hadn't projected much warmth.

'So what about you, Lauren? Did you have a happy childhood?'

Her smile was warm and wistful. 'Very.'

'In the house where you are living now?'

She nodded, having already told him how she had moved from London, where she'd lived for little more than a year, back to the farmhouse when she had taken on caring for Danny. It was then that she'd let out the stables and taken on the unmarried, intrepid Fiona to run them.

'And did you have any dreams or desires before you were forced into the role of guardian, beyond working on the checkout at your local garden centre, or typing house particulars in an estate agent's office?'

She remembered mentioning the estate agent's job on the night they had met, but not the reason for her being in London in the first place—not how hard she had been studying during her evenings and at weekends.

'Yes, I did,' she answered and, deciding to wipe out that glimmer of mockery in his devastating eyes, along with any more preconceived ideas he might have about her, added, 'I wanted to be a vet.'

He looked surprised, just as she'd thought he would.

'So why didn't you?' he enquired, frowning.

'My parents died during my first term at uni.' She gave a little shrug. 'So I left.'

'*Mamma mia!* I'd no idea!'

'That my parents were dead?' She couldn't believe he could have forgotten a thing like that. She couldn't imagine him ever forgetting anything.

'No, of course not.' Now it was his turn to sound slightly affronted. 'Only that you had lost them in such recent years. For some reason I imagined it was when you were a child...'

'I thought Angelo might have mentioned it,' she said. 'Vikki must have told him.' Or perhaps she hadn't, Lauren thought wildly, remembering with an aching regret how her sister had always seemed ashamed of her parents and her lowly origin.

'If she did, he didn't say anything to me. My brother and I communicated very little,' Emiliano said, 'and, when we did, it was seldom on a social footing. I am afraid that Angelo and I rarely saw eye to eye.'

There it was. Clarified. Everything she had suspected and speculated over.

'What did your parents do?' he enquired before she could ask him why.

'Mum wrote horoscopes. You know, star signs? For an astrology magazine. She believed every word of it.' Her mouth curved fondly as she thought about her gentle, often distracted mother, who had the ability to let every worldly care wash over her. 'She was unconventional in her ideas. Her views. In the way she dressed…' So much so, Lauren remembered, that she and her sister had often been the butt of some unkind teasing at school, although she had never minded quite as much as Vikki had.

'And your father?'

'He was a teacher. Well, a retired professor, really. Mum was a dropout student from the college where he taught. That's how they met. At some sort of reunion or other.'

'And what did he profess?'

'Natural sciences.' She grinned. 'And the whackiest ideas no one ever wanted to listen to!'

Emiliano smiled. 'They sound like characters.'

'They were.'

'What happened?' he prompted in a gentle tone.

'Mum got hold of an idea that she had an ancestor who really had mystical powers. Dad didn't actually believe most of what Mum wrote, but he adored her and supported her in everything she wanted to do.

They took a backpacking trip in South America on the trail of this mysterious ancestor. They never found one, but they caught a tropical fever for their trouble, and I lost *two* in the process.'

'I'm sorry.'

She made a dismissive little gesture with her hands. 'It happened.'

Emiliano's eyes were darkly reflective. 'And you would have been…how old at the time?'

When she told him, he said only, 'So you relinquished your career path to look after your sister, who would, no doubt, have been still at school.'

'I had to earn some money.'

'You have never told me this before,' he reproached softly.

He was right. But then she hadn't wanted to spin a sob story to a man she had only just met, reluctant as she had been to ruin the magic of those two days. When she'd mentioned losing her parents, she recalled saying that it had happened when she and Vikki were young. She hadn't wanted to talk about the past or to dwell on anything unhappy and, highly tuned as he was to the sensibilities of those around him, he hadn't pressed her for any more information.

'And you have never thought about going back?'

'To university?' She shrugged again. 'For a while I did, but financially it wasn't possible. I needed to live. And then…when Vikki…'

He nodded as her voice tailed off, obviously understanding how much it still hurt to talk about the accident.

'Of course.'

Quickly stemming emotion, she said, 'And now there are far more important things in life.'

Like caring for his nephew, Emiliano thought, shaken to the core by what she had told him—by the compromises she had had to make. He wondered how many more surprises this lovely young woman had in store for him, because it had suddenly dawned on him how little he knew about her, despite the past intimacies they had shared.

All he had wanted two years ago, he realised guiltily, was to get her into bed and to keep her there for as long as he wanted to amuse himself with her. It had driven his libido through the ceiling when he had discovered that all she seemed to want was to indulge him in his fantasy—which was to lose himself in that glorious body of hers as much as she wanted to lose herself in his.

He had bedded a gold-digger, he had thought that day he had heard her discussing him with her sister. Or had it been the other way round? He couldn't say with any certainty any more. But he had still been convinced she was a woman with a mission when he had turned up at her home and accused her of monopolising his brother's child. What he hadn't expected to find was a girl who rescued dogs and rubbed bumps on a toddler's knees, and who had been handed more than her fair share of responsibility at a very young age. Now he wanted to know more about her beyond the purely physical, he realised, startled even to be thinking it.

A simple gesture from him summoned a waiter to their table and a few minutes later he was settling the bill.

'Let's take a walk,' he said.

* * *

Lauren was far too conscious of Emiliano's dark attraction as they walked, without touching, along the waterfront and out onto the night-shrouded jetty.

Here lights twinkled on either side of the wooden structure, throwing back distorted reflections from the dark water. But the silence was like a mocking witness to the powerful sensuality that lay between them and, unable to cope with her screaming responses, Lauren tried to still them by asking, 'Why didn't you get along with your brother?'

His lips were pursed as he thought about it, his profile given added strength by the night shadows and the scant light from a fine sliver of new moon.

'Different personalities. Different temperaments.'

He wasn't saying that Angelo Cannavaro was a womanising gambler who thought that life was just a playing field for whatever pleasure took his fancy out of respect for his brother's memory—even if he was thinking it—and she admired him for that.

'He got on with your stepmother?' She had sensed that much on the night of the party, something her sister had later confirmed.

'He was only eight months old when she married my father and, as she already knew she couldn't have any children, she doted on him as if he were her own baby.'

'Indulged him, you mean.'

His lips moved in a wry gesture.

'So what about you?' Lauren asked.

'I was five. Self-willed and far too much for her to handle. A very intractable child.'

'I don't believe it!' she smiled. 'Wilful, maybe, with a mind of your own.'

'Always.'

'But not deliberately naughty.'

He merely shrugged at that.

'It must have been hard for you too. I mean…having another woman step into your birth mother's shoes.' She remembered reading somewhere that Marco Cannavaro had lost his first wife to cancer only two months after the birth of their second son, Angelo. What she hadn't known was that the boys' father had married again so soon.

'Do you remember her?' she asked Emiliano quietly, feeling for him.

'Surprisingly vividly,' he replied. 'The way her hair shone. Her smile. The way she smelled—although any memories of actually being with her are very vague. And, *sì*, my father *did* have an extra-marital affair and *did* marry his mistress, if that is what you are wondering,' he concluded, surprising her, because she had been, but had been far too prudent to ask.

'So how did she learn to cope? Your stepmother?' Lauren expanded.

'With boarding schools and vacations spent with a very strict maiden aunt, who wasn't actually an aunt at all, but my father's second cousin.'

'You mean you were sent away?' *Treated as if he wasn't one of the family?* 'Didn't your father mind?'

'He was happy just as long as Claudette was happy. He believed it would develop my powers of self-sufficiency and make me independent, and I suppose it did. It did not, however, help to bring us close as a family. And Angelo…' He made a sort of exasperated sound and a hopeless gesture with his hands, which somehow seemed to say everything that he couldn't. 'In the end I could do nothing except stand by and watch my brother destroy himself. Can you imagine how that makes me feel?'

'Yes,' Lauren empathised, with her heart going out to him, and realised now what he had meant at that party when he'd said he couldn't actually call himself a friend of the family. He'd had no family to speak of, she thought. Not one that cared. 'It makes you feel useless and self-recriminating and as though you've somehow desperately failed.'

They had never spoken like this before and his revelation had her opening up to him and unburdening herself of things she had never told a soul.

'When our parents died, I think that Vikki was angry with them for leaving her. She reacted by doing everything she knew she shouldn't. Staying out all night. Getting into bad company, drugs…You know the sort of thing. In the end I couldn't reason with her and I just let her walk away. I could have done more and I didn't. If I'd only concentrated less on myself and how I was going to get by and taken more interest in her, she might not have left and drifted so far away from all the values that Mum and Dad taught us. If I'd done more—'

'Don't,' Emiliano interrupted firmly, stopping dead and pulling her round to face him. 'You were little more than a child yourself, having to cope with what amounted to parental responsibility. At eighteen we are still learning to take responsibility for ourselves. You said you opted out of university and then gave up any idea of furthering your studies when you were left with Daniele to look after. Twice you have given up your career for your sister. Don't give up any more of your life by letting it be eroded by guilt. You have done a marvellous job, especially with our nephew. Given up so much…' He slid his fingers along her arm in a sensual caress. 'Which is why I could be excused, I think, for imagining you would want to take more of a back seat now and let someone else take the strain.'

'No!' She tried to pull away, but he had caught her by the hand. 'You don't understand! How can you?' she uttered, her words torn from her heart. 'When you didn't even have a family you were remotely close to? I've lost everyone I've ever loved!' Tears were threatening, burning her eyes, but she refused to let him see them fall. 'I can't lose Danny too! Not to you. Not to anyone! I can't and I *won't* give him up!'

She looked away from him, at the blur of lights along the walkway over which they had just come, ashamed of the tears that had triumphed.

'Maybe I didn't understand. But I think I'm beginning to,' she heard Emiliano saying heavily as he cupped her cheek in the palm of his hand and gently turned her face to his.

He was the enemy, she thought. The one person who could destroy her very world. Yet even the simplest touch from him had the power to set her pulse racing, and with no strength now to resist him she turned her tear-streaked face into his warm palm.

As if that were the only signal he had been waiting for, he wound an arm around her middle and caught her against the pulsing strength of his body.

Sensations flooded through her like the night sounds were flooding the air—the distant steel band, the chirruping crickets, the muted laughter from the bar and its happy couples along the far side of the wharf.

She didn't care what they must look like as Emiliano's mouth came down over hers, only visualising their dark silhouettes as she leaned into him with all the desire she had kept locked tightly inside her since that wild afternoon on the beach the day after they had arrived.

His hands ran over her body with a possessiveness that left her weak and wanting—wanting him like she had never wanted anyone or anything in her life.

She wanted to resist, but she didn't know how to.

'Come to bed with me,' he whispered against her hair, and she was lost.

CHAPTER SIX

'WHERE ARE WE going?' Lauren asked as they came back along the jetty and onto the wharf, not separately now, but with Emiliano's arm locking her to his side. 'The car's in that direction.' She was pointing back towards the bar.

'So is home. And about an hour's drive away.' There was exciting purpose to his face, illuminated by the lights along the quayside. 'But I don't think I—that either of us—can wait that long.'

Lauren looked at him questioningly, her excitement rising with her heightening anticipation.

From this distance the music and laughter from the bar had all but diminished, the only immediate sounds now the slap-slop of Lauren's flip-flops on the concrete over Emiliano's soft-soled, almost silent tread, and the creak of cooling timber and chink of metal from the moored boats with the water lapping against their hulls.

'Where are we going?' she asked again, more huskily this time, after he brought her along another jetty and was handing her down into an inflatable black dinghy, the same one, she was sure, she had seen being brought to shore earlier in the evening.

'To bed,' he answered uninformatively after he had stepped in beside her and started the engine, but there was laughter in his voice as he added, 'Where else?'

The yacht they were racing towards was the one she had seen come in when they had been sitting at that restaurant table, and Lauren's mouth dropped open as Emiliano brought the dinghy alongside the steps at its impressive stern.

'This is *yours*!' she exclaimed, with her jaw dropping open. A sleek white vessel of eye-popping proportions, she remembered thinking how it would need the skill of a fully trained crew to handle it.

He didn't answer. He was addressing two male members of his crew who, wearing black T-shirts and built like rugby forwards, had appeared on the platform above them. Emiliano was conversing with them in his own language and, apart from a curt nod from each of the men that acknowledged Lauren's presence as Emiliano helped her aboard, they went about dealing with the vacated dinghy.

'Can I get you anything?' he offered as he guided her through a pair of glass doors into the boat's luxurious interior.

Only a minute to recover from what I should have expected! she thought, struck by an immediate impression of soft leather and polished maple and carpets that seemed to swallow her underfoot. Yet she hadn't even dreamed that this yacht could be his when she'd seen it arrive.

When she shook her head, he said, 'In that case...' He was gesturing towards the stairs leading to what was clearly the sleeping quarters and Lauren's pulse-rate soared.

'I feel like a pirate's bounty!' Ahead of him, she laughed nervously over her shoulder with her stomach doing funny things because it was easy to imagine his dark Latin face scarred by plunder and pillage, his bare contoured chest gleaming as he plucked an unsuspecting maiden from some unfortunate vessel he had just claimed as his own.

'A pirate, mmm...' His smile was feral and his eyes didn't leave hers as he opened the door to what was obviously the master cabin. 'Is that how you see me?'

Lauren had to stifle a gasp at the sheer opulence of the room.

Dark, highly polished surfaces reflected the soft light given off by state-of-the-art wall-lamps, and this room too was thickly carpeted in pale cream to match the cream and black curtains and cushions scattered around the cabin and over the creamy satin coverlet on the king-size bed.

Had he planned this? If he had, she didn't think she wanted to know.

'I see you as devious,' she murmured, keeping her fanciful thinking of a few moments ago purely to herself.

He laughed as he waited for her to precede him. 'I'm not sure I like that.'

'You aren't supposed to,' she told him with a sudden dryness in her throat as she heard the door click closed behind them, shutting out the world.

She was in his world now—and his alone—captured like a moth in the all-consuming heat of a dangerous flame.

'Wow!' she expressed, overawed by his wealth and power and a lifestyle that mere mortals like her could only dream about. 'When you take a woman to bed— you take her to *bed!*'

'So come to bed.' His voice was sensuously soft from just behind her.

Glancing back, she saw him holding out his hand.

'What are you thinking? Wondering?' he asked, coming silently over the carpet towards her. 'How many other women I might have...*ravished*—' it was said with deliberate emphasis '—in this room?'

Faint colour touched her cheeks because she had been.

'None,' he murmured, surprising her with that declaration. 'It's a corporate yacht, which I am having delivered to Barbados as a conference vessel. So if you are looking for...What is it they call them in English? Ah, yes! Notches,' he remembered, smiling, 'on my metaphorical bedpost, I am afraid you will not find any here.'

Relieved to know that, much more than she'd expected to be, Lauren gave him a tense little smile. She had known him so intimately and yet, despite what he had said, the thought of all those other, far more sophisticated women he must have known—whether on land or off it—when she hadn't had so much as a casual fling with anyone since that embarrassing episode with him in the past, had her suddenly fearing that she might disappoint him now.

'Emiliano...' Her eyes were resting on his, her green irises, like that one word, laid bare with longing.

'Don't say anything,' he whispered, and closed the distance between them.

His body was like a rock she could only cling to as she gave herself up to the blinding passion of his kiss. But it was a passion that matched hers, and she pressed her body closer to his, close enough to recognise every tensing muscle as he caught her hard against his warm and dominating strength.

His hands were moving over her as though they couldn't get enough of her, while their mutual breathing came hard and fast and their mouths fused and separated and met again with a hunger that made Lauren cry out from the intensity of her need.

'Easy,' Emiliano breathed, drawing back a little, slowing down the pace. 'We have all night for this and I want to savour every moment I can with you, *cara mia.*'

Until it was over? *They* were over? She didn't even want to think about that.

'Emiliano...'

'What is it?' he prompted, sensing her hesitation, the slight change in her mood.

'I'm...not protected,' she murmured, feeling almost ashamed to be admitting it.

'You don't need to be,' he reassured her, which obviously meant that he would take care of things. 'Unless, of course, you are having second thoughts about sleeping with me,' he suggested softly, 'in which case I shall have to respect your wishes and order my crew to go full steam ahead.'

And always see her as—at worst—a tease? And at best someone fickle? Unsure of what she wanted? When it was him she was unsure of? When she was afraid of getting hurt?

'No!' She said it a little too quickly, desperate as

she was to keep him with her and, trying to be like one of those sophisticated women who didn't mind when the time came to leave his bed, in a soft demand she breathed, 'Take off your clothes.'

He laughed softly, catching one of the hands stroking his chest in the comparatively dark grasp of his. 'Why don't you do it for me?' he invited silkily.

He had said those words to her before, when she'd suggested he bathe his wound after he'd helped her untangle Brutus, and the memory of how he'd appeared, like a dark rescuer out of nowhere, filled her with an overwhelming intensity of emotion.

Even so, she had never undressed a man before, even over those crazy two days when they had been as intimate as any couple could be, and nervously she brought her tongue across her top lip.

Now, controlling her trembling fingers, she started slipping the buttons of his shirt, loving the way his breathing deepened with every inch of bronzed chest she exposed.

'You've done this before,' he murmured heavily and with deep-sounding satisfaction.

Laughing tensely, Lauren said, 'Oh, yes. Many times!' And knew from the faint smile that touched his mouth that he wasn't fooled.

Right then, though, she didn't care if he believed it or not. All she wanted was to please him and for him not to realise that there had been no one in her life that she had come remotely close to making love with since she had encountered his unforgettable and tutoring skill. No one who had ever made her feel like he did—ever!

Slipping her hands inside his shirt, she pushed the

light fabric off his shoulders. His flesh was warm and satin-smooth beneath her fingers and a little frisson ran through her from actually being able to touch him like this again.

His groan seemed to reverberate from his chest as she pressed her lips against it, inhaling the stirring fragrance of his masculine cologne and that other more personal scent that was wholly his. More boldly then, she ran her tongue along the valley of his sternum, allowing it to stray across first one flat, dark masculine nipple and then the other.

'I think it only fair to tell you, darling. There are rules in this cabin.' His chest rose and fell heavily beneath its smattering of dark hair. 'Captain's orders,' he outlined, his voice gravelly, husky. 'Whatever you do to me, *mia cara*, I will do to you.'

A sensually inspired little laugh escaped her. Oh, he was clever!

With her hands splayed against his flesh, she pressed her cheek against the cushioning pillow of his chest, then tilted her face to his with tantalising eyes before turning back to claim one tight masculine nipple with her mouth.

He groaned again, sounding almost in pain from the pleasure it gave him.

'I never knew you liked that,' she whispered, surprised.

'How could I not like anything you do t—' His words were broken by the shivering breath he dragged in, his fingers twisting in the wild tumble of her hair.

Excitement drove her on, licking and nipping his chest, his ribcage and his hard lean flanks, the feel and scent and taste of him exciting her as much as the sensual tensing of his body as her kisses continued to descend, caress, explore.

His waist was firm and tight beneath her fingers and, like the rest of his long frame, without an ounce of surplus flesh to mar its perfection.

'I'm warning you,' he promised as she slid the zip of his trousers, but made no attempt to stop her in her determination to please him.

'You're amazing,' she whispered when he stood there in his unashamed nakedness. A huge hunting animal. Comfortable with the way nature had made him. Dominant. Predatory. And aroused!

His thighs were heavily muscled and felt like silk-sheathed granite beneath her fingers. He tasted slightly salty against her tongue...

His breath shuddered violently through him as though it were almost too much to bear. The next instant he pulled sharply away from her with his face flushed and his eyes tightly closed as he battled for control.

'And now it's my turn,' he breathed with heart-stopping determination, drawing a gasp from her when he suddenly lifted her off her feet. 'Don't worry. It is perfectly soundproofed,' he assured her, aware of the concerned glance she shot towards the cabin door. 'A pirate needs privacy when he's savouring his bounty. And am I going to savour mine, *carissima*.'

Wild responses leaped through her from the determined purpose in his voice, stirring a breathless excitement in her as she felt the mattress on the big bed depress beneath their joint weight.

With his hair falling forward, he was lying across her, this man who was both a sophisticate and an untamed animal, and the combination of the two was incredibly arousing.

Closing her eyes, measuring him only with her tactile senses, she revelled in the perfect structure of bone and muscle, of hair-coarsened velvet and smooth satin over iron and steel.

'Emiliano...'

She whispered his name as his hands ran over the flimsy fabric of her dress, and that was an unbelievable turn-on too because he seemed in no hurry to undress her.

Her body rose to meet the warmth of the hand skimming over her breast, over the dip of her waist and the curve of her hip. But when it touched the apex of her thighs she bucked convulsively towards him, inviting the ultimate contact. Needing it. Craving *him* like an addict.

Ignoring her silent supplication, he let his fingers trail along the length of one smooth silken leg and then the other, before drawing his hand away to repeat the same exquisite torment all over again.

'Please...' Her nails grazed along the warm, flexing muscles of his back. 'Oh, please, Emiliano,' she begged.

She was pleading because of him, because of what he was doing to her, he realised, with his masculine pride swelling.

'What is it?' His eyelids were heavy with desire, but there was sensual teasing in his voice too. 'What is it you want, *carissima*?'

'You know very well.' Her tone was lightly scolding and her green eyes were darkened from the depths of her need.

'Oh, this…'

When he slipped the thin straps off her shoulders, pulling the dress down over her breasts and the gentler curve of her hips, the sight of her beautiful body, with the way those lovely breasts moved as she wriggled to make it easier for him to remove it, seemed to suck the air out of Emilano's lungs.

'*Mia bella…*' He had had his share of beautiful women, but never one so perfectly tantalising or so sensitive to his touch. Sensitive emotionally, too, he was beginning to appreciate, wondering how he could ever have been so wrong about her, misjudging her character so completely. In the world he moved in, he couldn't afford to make mistakes about people. And yet he had, he realised, much to his disconcertion and his shame.

But she was whimpering softly just from the slide of his hand across her ribcage, offering him the beautiful gift of her body as she had done so many times before.

He moved across her now, feeling like a king rather than a plunderer when he saw her eyelids grow heavy as he fondled her tender breasts, feeding on her soft moans of pleasure when he drew each perfect pale orb into his mouth in turn.

Her skin felt like silk, he thought, finding her whole body as soft and yielding as his own was hard. She was ready for him, he realised, as she writhed beneath him and her legs splayed wider like butterfly wings wanting to soak up the sun. But he had promised her everything and he was never a man to renege on a promise, he reminded himself. And then, with a mentally wicked smile—no matter how much of a punishment it might be for him to keep it!

He heard her breathing quicken in anticipation as his lips moved over the taut plane of her abdomen, and when his mouth found that most secret part of her she gave a shuddering gasp of pleasure.

She hadn't been a virgin when they had come together first but, from the way she had responded to him and was responding to him now, making him feel as if he was the only man in the universe, she might only ever have been his, and suddenly he couldn't bear the thought of any other man making love to her.

It filled him with such momentary possessiveness that he knew a sudden atavistic desire to impregnate her. To stamp his mark on her and watch her middle grow big with his child. Their child. The thought of entering her unprotected and feeling nothing but her soft warm flesh around him produced an ache in his body that almost made him lose control.

But she wouldn't welcome such reckless behaviour from him. Oh, perhaps to begin with! he thought, while they were both driven by their mutual hunger and need for each other. But not later, when she realised the implications of what they had done. Besides, they had Daniele, and he already loved the infant as if he were his own. How could he not? he thought distractedly, when his brother's blood flowed in the child's veins and bound him to Daniele, just as it bound Lauren to him, connected her to him irrevocably—whether she wanted to accept that or not.

Breathing raggedly, she lay unmoving with her eyes closed as he withdrew a little to do what he had to do. Then he moved over her again and, parting her thighs with gentle fingers, positioned himself above her before sinking deeply into her.

She cried out from the pleasure that echoed his own throaty growl as he lifted her hips to meet his with each increasingly deep surge of his body.

She started to climax almost at once, only a second before he gave one final driving thrust and felt his seed exploding out of him.

Shuddering with release, he collapsed against her, his breathing heavy, his body throbbing while she gripped him tightly with each contraction of her eager body, holding him there, high up in the cushioning warmth of her femininity.

It was only just dawn as the yacht brought them towards the cove below Emiliano's house, but he had promised Lauren the previous night that they would be back before Daniele awoke.

It was a brand new vessel, Emiliano had told her, which he had purchased in Florida on his last visit, and which he had had diverted from its planned route by the very efficient Italian crew he had employed.

'So you did plan it!' Lauren chided softly after they had come up on deck to watch the sun as it rose above the lush vegetation spilling down to the aquamarine water. 'Was this all part of your scheme when you warned me I'd be coming out with you the other night?'

'Not at all. And there certainly was no scheme,' he assured her firmly. 'My original plan was to have them bring it straight here before taking it to Barbados, but I didn't realise it was so close to the island until my skipper rang me just before dinner last night to let me know they were ready to bring the vessel in. I thought it would be a surprise and particularly enjoyable for you if they changed course and picked us up from the lagoon, so that I could give you a starlit cruise back to the house last night instead of returning by road.'

Just like that! Lauren realised, amazed by how effortlessly things worked when you were as rich and important as Emiliano. And naturally the car would be returned to the house as if by magic too!

'Having you spend the night in my bed was an unexpected bonus that I certainly did not plan.'

'Well, you definitely made the journey home particularly enjoyable!' she laughed with a delicious little shiver running through her. She was still basking in the aftermath of a night spent in his arms, and one or two tender places on her body certainly bore lingering mementoes of their passionate lovemaking.

'And what did you mean by my *warning* you that I was intending to take you out?' he enquired, pretending to look put out by her remark. 'I think I was the one in the greatest danger last night, *mia cara*. It had to be the first time in my life that I found myself alone with a woman who *ordered* me to take off my clothes.'

'I hadn't realised you were so deprived!' she laughed, with her stomach doing a somersault from remembering how magnificent he had looked in his nakedness and, in particular, had felt, beneath her caressing fingers. 'If I'd known, I would have been far, far more adventurous with you!'

Laughing with her, he said, 'What are you doing? Trying to tempt me, *mia bella*? I have sixty-five feet of hull I need to steer into that cove,' he reminded her, confirming that even though he had entirely competent employees to do the job for him, there were al-

ways some things that he just had to do for himself.
'However...' the sun struck his slim gold watch as he
crooked his arm to consult it '...we are not there yet.'
Laughter lit his eyes, which were shining with an almost amber fire because of the dazzling reflections
bouncing off the water. But they were burning with
another kind of fire too, Lauren noted excitedly, as he
said, grabbing her hand, 'Which means you will just
have enough time left, *cara mia*, to show me exactly
how...adventurous you can be.'

It was the first time he had given her carte blanche
to please him without any intervention from him, she
thought, as she lay with him in the luxurious cabin,
knowing he was a man who usually liked to take control.

But now she delighted in his voluntary and totally
uninhibited surrender as she watched his long lashes
feather down against the wells of his eyes, and his forehead groove in tortured ecstasy as she brought every
ounce of sexual tension ebbing from him in the most
intimate and pleasurable way.

Later, lying with her hair spread like flaming silk
across his chest, Lauren stretched languorously like a
contented she-cat and, bringing her arms down, murmured, 'Was that adventurous enough for you?'

He didn't even open his eyes as she raised herself up
on an elbow. Instead, he simply breathed in response,
'It is rather soon to tell. I think we will just have to try
that again some time.'

Laughing softly, Lauren ran her hand over the crisp
hair of his chest. He was beautiful, she thought, gazing down at him. He made love to her with so much

passion, and yet so much consideration too, taking his time, putting her pleasure first, which made him an exciting and incredible lover.

She wondered how anyone who had known such indifference in their childhood could have matured into such a well-balanced, thoughtful and attentive man. She had told him last night that she had lost everyone who mattered to her. But at least she had known she was loved and cared for, while he…

He had lost his mother so young, she reflected, with her heart going out to him. And then, not just his father, but his brother too, when he had been shut out of the family on the whim of an uncaring stepmother. It was hardly surprising, therefore, that he wanted Daniele, she realised, understanding now. The toddler was the only blood relative he had left to hang on to. The only survivor of a family where everyone else had let him down.

Her heart ached for him so much that it actually hurt.

I love him, she thought, in the instant that he opened his eyes.

'What is it, *cara*?' His forehead pleated with concern as he ran a hand along her arm to the smooth curve of her naked shoulder. 'Is something troubling you? You are not regretting it, no?'

He meant the whole night and the stage their relationship had now reached. But what stage had they reached? Lauren wondered anxiously. From Emiliano's point of view, she was probably just another willing partner who had agreed to share his bed, while she…

She had recklessly and very unwisely turned that corner she had nearly turned two years ago after only a matter of hours in his bed and fallen hopelessly in love with him. But, unlike before, she now knew so much more about him—knew the pain and the very complex issues that had made him the man he was. She also knew that this time there could be no turning back

'No, of course not,' she replied, because whatever happened from now on, she knew she would love him for ever and that, no matter what he said or did, she would live on the memory of her time on this yacht with him for the rest of her life.

CHAPTER SEVEN

'SO TELL ME about Stephen,' Emiliano suggested casually a couple of days later as they reclined under a large green parasol on the beach below the house.

'Stephen?' Lauren echoed, frowning. They were sharing the same luxuriously padded sun lounger and Lauren was leaning back with her head resting against his bare chest. In nothing but a pair of navy blue swimming trunks, his body felt warm and smelled deliciously masculine. 'Oh, Stephen!' He had asked her about him that day when he had helped her untangle Brutus from the wire, and she remembered taking a warped pleasure out of withholding what he really wanted to know. 'Why?' She was glancing up at him over her shoulder, her green eyes twinkling wickedly. 'Are you jealous?'

'If I have reason to be after what we have been doing over the past few days,' he commented with mock sternness, 'then obviously I have not been doing my job properly.'

'Then you'll just have to practise more,' she purred with a sensuous little wriggle and earned herself a firm tightening of his arm across her middle.

'Tell me what he means to you,' he insisted.

He sounded deadly serious now and she knew it was time to stop teasing him.

'He means everything to me—when I've run out of eggs,' she couldn't resist saying nevertheless. 'Or if Danny and I are desperate for some milk on our porridge. So does his wife of thirty years. Or even one of his older sons. As long as there's somebody serving in the dairy.'

'You little…' He left the noun hanging with a promise of some delightful pay-back.

Sitting beside them on the sand under a smaller matching parasol, Daniele was demolishing a fort that she and Emiliano had made for him earlier. Now, looking up at them, his little spade suspended in mid-bash, he gave them both a cheeky grin before resuming his demolition job.

'What about you?' she asked tentatively. 'Do you have someone like a Stephen—or should I say a Stephanie—stashed away somewhere?'

'Not at present,' he drawled, stroking her hair back off her shoulder so he could tease the soft skin he had exposed with a spine-shivering caress of his tongue. 'Not even one I could claim supplies me with eggs.'

Lauren's tense little laugh was broken by another sensual shudder as his long fingers slid ever so subtly under the band of the little white triangle spanning her lower body.

Not at present, he had said. Did that mean that there was likely to be someone in the near future? she wondered, a little deflated.

She couldn't dwell on that, though, not when his teeth were nipping the sensitive area at the juncture of her neck and shoulder, and his other hand had come up under her breast, supporting, yet not actually claiming its full swell in its palm.

Frustration was a torment that had her wriggling again and quietly groaning this time. Her breast was aching for him to reach a little higher and drag his thumb across it, while her femininity craved for him to slide those skilled fingers further inside her bikini briefs. But she knew he wouldn't—that they couldn't—take things any further with Danny there.

'You know...lying in the sun seems to make you incredibly sexy,' Emiliano remarked, bringing his lower hand up to rest casually—at least casually where *he* was concerned, Lauren thought, tingling with need—across her abdomen. She noticed how dark his splayed fingers were across her comparatively paler flesh, like hard bronze against the softer, more malleable gold.

'The sun?' Her breathing came a little more shallowly than it had a few moments ago. 'Perhaps it's an aphrodisiac. Or perhaps it has something to do with you.'

Suddenly she realised what this little game of sensual torment was all about. She had been teasing him about Stephen, and women didn't tease men like Emiliano Cannavaro in that way and get away with it.

'No, *carissima*.' His endearment was huskily spoken, the flick of his tongue exquisite torture across the sensitive chamber of her ear. 'It has very little to do with me.'

That last word coincided with the depression of his hand against her tummy, an action so arousing that she let out a small shocked gasp from the sharp contraction it produced at the very core of her femininity.

'I'm going in.' She sat up quickly, trembling, breath-

less. 'Will you bring Danny back?' She was already
on her feet, burning up with sexual frustration. 'Or
shall I take him?' She only knew she couldn't stay
there another minute.

'I'll bring him back,' he drawled.

Whether he was affected by what he had been doing
to her, she wasn't sure. She was too disconcerted to
look at him as she grabbed her small beach bag and
started back over the sand, seeking only the calming
atmosphere inside the house and the merciful isolation of her own room.

The cool water of the shower did little to ease her
frustration. The crests of her breasts were peaked beneath the application of the shower gel, and her very
womb felt as if it were aching from the promises it
had been denied.

You wait! Emiliano Cannavaro, she promised in return, wondering how big a fool she was being for loving him. Yet it wasn't his deliberate attempt to frustrate
her out there that was making her angry to the point
of tears. It was because of that moment when she had
asked him in a roundabout way if there was anyone
that *she* should be jealous of, and he had answered
simply, 'Not at present'!

What was she supposed to deduce from that? she
asked herself. That he was currently between girl-
friends and would be taking up with someone else
the minute he'd finished amusing himself with her?

She didn't hear the door to the bathroom open, or
the door to the shower cubicle, so that when she turned
round and saw Emiliano stepping in beside her she
gave a gasp of shocked surprise.

'That was not very kind of me, was it?' he admit-

ted with a self-effacing grimace. 'But one thing you
will grow to learn about me, *cara mia*, is that if ever I
make mistakes, I always believe in putting them right.'

Which put him there. With her. And naked! she realised with shuddering pleasure as he drew her against
him.

But it was what he had just said: those five words—
you will grow to learn—that seemed to wash away her
despondency, in the same way his hard, warm body
was promising to wash away her aching need. Didn't
they imply that she would be part of his life for a while
at least? That he didn't intend just to throw her over
for someone else the instant these few glorious weeks
with him were over?

She couldn't think any more because his mouth had
swooped and was covering hers and all she wanted was
to be with him like this. Today. Here and now!

And now it was *his* hands that were lathering her
breasts, driving her demented with longing as he caressed their aching fullness, teasing their blossoming
buds with infinite skill.

His mouth was hard and hungry—as hungry as hers
was for his insistent and deepening kiss.

The slipperiness of their wet bodies was unbelievably erotic, the gel with which he had been massaging
her making his flesh as slick as hers.

Lauren's hands moved over the thrilling musculature of his back, the unleashed power she could feel
pulsing beneath his firm flesh making her crave ful-
filment as she had never craved it before.

If he didn't love her soon she would die of wanting!

But he was as desperate as she was, she realised,
as he forced her back against the tiles and it was with

only a mild distraction that she realised he was already prepared.

Clutching at his shoulders, she swayed towards him as he guided himself into her wet and willing body and then, with one powerful thrust, drove deeply into her, making her cry out as her body shuddered with spiralling pleasure.

She had never made love standing up before, let alone under the relentless jets of a shower. The whole experience heightened her arousal as he pushed even more deeply into her, driving them both into a wild rhythm of sensation that was as swift as it was hot, and which brought them, collapsing and breathless when it was over, against the luxurious marble tiles of the cubicle.

It had been by tacit agreement that she had progressed from her own beautiful room at the back of the house to the understated luxury of the master suite with its polished cedar furniture and richly patterned furnishings, since once Emiliano had had her in his bed, he was, it seemed, unequivocally determined to keep her there.

'You are where you belong, *mia bella*. Accept it,' he had said to her when she expressed her concern over what Constance and the rest of his staff might think. 'Constance has three robust sons who did not arrive on this planet through wishful thinking. And I think by now, *cara*, that my employees would think it very strange if you were not sharing my bed.'

So that told her, Lauren thought, wishing she could adopt the same nonchalant attitude. But she wasn't as worldly or as free-thinking and casual about sex as he seemed to be, and she guessed that that was part of her problem: having people assume that she was happy to be merely a diversion—a sex toy—in the bed of a man who clearly didn't love her.

Also, since that night on the wharf, before he'd taken her to his yacht, he hadn't said another word about Daniele's future.

Was she living in a fool's paradise? she wondered then, and again that same evening when they had been in the salon listening to one of Emiliano's blues albums—which surprisingly she had grown to love—and she'd heard Etta James belting out something about rather losing her sight than watching the man she loved walk out of her life.

Well, I wouldn't go that far, Etta. But you're close, she'd thought achingly, and had taken herself off to bed, where she'd pretended to be asleep when Emiliano joined her.

It was earlier than usual when she awoke, and Emiliano's side of the bed was deserted.

Taking a quick shower in the master bedroom's luxurious en suite bathroom which, though not necessarily more splendidly appointed, was nearly twice the size of her own, Lauren donned a strapless white sundress with an elasticated top before going along the landing to check on Daniele.

Finding his room deserted, and craving a fruity drink, she made her way quickly downstairs to the large and sunny kitchen which, despite all its up-to-the-minute equipment and stainless steel appliances, still managed to maintain a very welcoming feel.

Wearing a white short-sleeved shirt and tie teemed with light suit trousers Emiliano was leaning against one of the counters, browsing through a newspaper.

Daniele was already in his high chair with a half-eaten piece of papaya in front of him. His eyes were fixed on the wall-mounted television beside the huge refrigerator, which was showing a local programme about underwater exploration.

'*Buongiorno,*' Emiliano greeted her softly, closing his newspaper. 'I trust you slept well.' Those all-seeing eyes of his were tugging over her dress as though he knew she was wearing nothing but a skimpy brief beneath it. 'After...'

'Yes,' Lauren said quickly because, for all her pretending last night, she hadn't been able to sleep at all at first, a fact he had soon become wise to and had swiftly and effectively done something about. Apart from which, Constance had just emerged from the walk-in larder.

Returning her warm greeting, yet needing a diversion from her suddenly racing thoughts, Lauren went over and kissed Daniele's dark, downy head.

'Hello, darling.' She picked up the small succulent piece of yellow fruit from his plate and popped it into his mouth. 'What are you doing in the kitchen?' Normally he would have had his breakfast in the nursery, or out on the terrace with her.

'Vega!' Daniele said excitedly, pointing at the screen.

'He was restless,' Emiliano explained, laying his folded newspaper on the counter, 'so I brought him down with me so that he wouldn't disturb you.'

Like a father would, Lauren thought, impressed. Or a caring husband...

'Vega!' Daniele exclaimed again, dragging her

thoughts back from the unwise direction they had taken as he patted her arm to gain her attention.

'What is this "Vega"?' Emiliano asked, his baffled gaze following his nephew's to the colourful coral reef on the screen.

'Vega's his goldfish. Well, one of them,' Lauren explained. 'He calls every fish he sees now "Vega".'

'You name your *goldfish*?' Amusement laced his voice as he exchanged a conspiratorial glance with his housekeeper. They enjoyed a particularly good rapport, Lauren had noted, almost enviously, from day one.

'Where I come from fish is for eat'n,' Constance proclaimed in her lyrical island dialect as she busied herself with checking cupboards for necessary provisions.

'And do they all have names?' Emiliano directed at Lauren, still looking amused.

'We've only got three. And yes…' She paused before adding, 'The other two are Altair and Deneb.'

'Ex*cuse* me?' He was leaning back against the worktop, muscles bunching in his folded arms, a quizzical expression on his face.

'They make up the Summer Triangle,' she told him, wishing he didn't look quite so darn sexy, and not caring that he might think her daft. 'The three brightest stars in the night sky. In the northern hemisphere, that is.'

'Of course.'

'In summer.'

'Naturally.'

'You're laughing at me!' she accused, trying very hard now not to mind.

'No, I'm not.' But he was still chuckling and she

could hear stifled snorts of laughter coming from the direction of one of the cupboards.

'Yes, you are.'

'So how did you come by this…illustrious trio?'

His eloquent use of English—with barely any hesitation—never ceased to surprise her, even though it tumbled from his lips with that honey-thick accent of his that always sent delicious little quivers along her spine.

'I rescued them from a neighbour whose pond had a hole in it.'

He laughed out loud at that.

'The lining broke!' She stood there with her hands flung out, looking mildly exasperated. 'What's funny about that?'

'Nothing.' He was shaking his head, but was unable to keep a straight face.

Across the kitchen, she heard a cupboard door bang closed, unsuccessful in its deliberate attempt to disguise another uncontrolled squeak from Constance.

'You are very fascinating, Lauren Westwood.' Unfolding his arms, Emiliano came away from the worktop. 'As well as funny, caring and…' he closed the distance between them to touch a finger to her freckle-dusted nose before adding, and for her ears only '…delightfully sexy.'

With her pulse racing, she tossed him an upward glance that said he wasn't getting off that lightly. 'But wacky with it.'

'I didn't say that. Besides, what is this "wacky"?' His dark eyes were alive with teasing. He smelled good too, like the sea and the sand and the freshness of cut lemons with that first burst of zest.

Acting like someone who has been hit over the head! A fool, she defined mentally. The type of fool who had fallen in love with a man who was far too dangerous for her to handle.

'They aren't exactly my idea of a pet. I just got them for Danny,' she justified, 'so we had to give them names. And as I'd been watching a programme about the universe the previous night…' Naming those shimmering little bodies after stars had seemed appropriate. That was what she had been trying to say. She didn't tell him that, in doing so, it had felt like a way of commemorating her mother, in case he suspected her of following in Sophie Westwood's maternal footsteps with fortune-telling inclinations when nothing could have been further from the truth.

He was consulting his watch, though, and now he moved lithely across to the high chair.

'*Ciao, piccolo,*' he said, ruffling the toddler's soft hair, an affectionate gesture that tugged sharply at Lauren's heartstrings. 'You be a good *bambino*, eh?'

As Daniele looked up at his uncle and grinned, she could see Emiliano in him, from that increasing dark hair to what promised one day to be a definite proud tilt to his head, even though the little boy had inherited his mother's blue eyes and was, as yet, displaying more Westwood features than Cannavaro.

'You're going out?' The regretful note escaped Lauren before she could control it, although she should have realised immediately that he was. He didn't dress like that just to lounge around the pool all day!

'Disappointment, Lauren?' From over the baby's chair, the mouth that had plundered her shamelessly

last night was firming in cool satisfaction. 'Things
are looking up.'

With a word of thanks to his housekeeper, a jerk of
his chin towards the door indicated to Lauren that he
wanted to speak to her alone.

Checking that Daniele was still preoccupied with
his underwater world and not about to wail at being
left, she accompanied Emiliano into the wide, airy hall.

Its cedar doors stood open onto its marble-pillared
façade and the sunlight was flooding in across the ex-
quisitely tiled floor, spilling over some exotic plants
that stood in large pots near the doors and promising
another eternally glorious day.

'I would have taken you with me,' he stated, 'but it
is not feasible or possible. First I will be having breakfast with some officials from the council, and then I
am addressing a Fair Trade and Tourism conference.
Very interesting, but only for the invited, I am afraid.'

Of course. His speech, Lauren remembered.

'I will, however, be returning before dinner and
tonight, *mia cara*, there is something we must talk
about.'

The breeze through the open doors was ruffling his
hair and stirring the clattering spindles of an ornamen-
tal palm tree growing near the house.

'Is it about Danny?' Lauren returned hastily. 'Because if it is—'

'No. Not Danny,' he replied. Then, changing his
mind, he said, 'Well, *sì*. It is. Of course it is, in a—'

His mouth came down over hers before she could
cut in over whatever it was he had been going to say.

So this was it, she thought numbly. Reckoning time.
He had had his fun with her and now it was time to get

down to the real issue. Custody of Daniele. The only reason why she was there.

Emiliano…she tried to say, but his mouth was turning tender, insistent yet enslaving, and his hands were holding her head, his fingers thrust into the tumbling fire of her hair. But what could she say, she thought hopelessly, that he wouldn't try and argue against? Or try and make a claim to take Danny away from her? He had her where he wanted her, didn't he? And he knew how powerless she was to resist him—or anything about him—when he did this to her.

So where did that leave her? she thought, with her arms around his neck and her body shaping itself to the hard domination of his even though her mind rejected it. Where? Submitting, that was where. Giving in to him and whatever he demanded of her—whether she wanted to or not!

He broke the kiss only when she was like a malleable doll in his arms. His to do whatever he wanted with…

She couldn't even look at him as he said with marked determination and surprising formality, 'I think, Signorina Westwood, that we need a resolution here.'

He sounded impatient and slightly breathless, Lauren noted, trembling still from his drugging kiss as he reached around her for his jacket and the briefcase she hadn't even noticed standing on the padded cushion of a cane chair. Then, as he was turning to walk away, 'I think we should get married,' he said.

Emiliano didn't return for dinner that evening as promised.

After declining Constance's offer to put Daniele to

bed and doing it herself, Lauren curled up in the salon on one of the long corner sofas and browsed through a magazine on Caribbean culture, which she'd found lying on one of the glass-topped coffee tables beside her. Two hours later, when Emiliano still hadn't come home, she took herself off for a contemplative walk along the beach.

Did he have such little regard for her feelings that he could treat what had amounted to a proposal of sorts as nothing worth getting excited about and just walk away? she wondered, kicking up sand in the gathering dusk with her pumps.

If he had meant it.

A cloud of despondency settled over her at the possibility that he hadn't. That it might have been just an aside. A throwaway remark.

It hadn't helped her spirits when the conference he had been attending had been featured on the news earlier that evening and had shown Emiliano speaking on the subject of tourism, as well as fair trade. Another clip had shown him standing outside the building afterwards with one of the officials who had invited him to speak. Not a seasoned masculine official, as Lauren would have expected, but a model-slim Caribbean beauty who was scarcely much older than Emiliano, and who, she had noted reluctantly, from the way the woman had kept looking at him, could have put the 'i' in 'interest' where her celebrated Italian speaker was concerned.

The dinghy that had been beached for some days at the end of the cove had gone now, on the yacht that was anchored a little way offshore, all set for its journey to Barbados the following day. Above it, a solitary star was twinkling in the darkening sky.

Standing there, looking up at it, on the far curve of the cove, Lauren's only consolation was in knowing that men like Emiliano Cannavaro didn't make idle comments, nor say things they didn't actually mean.

'Well... Can you tell me what that one is called?'

Above the soothing wash of the waves over the night-shrouded beach, his voice drifted towards her, low and softly mocking.

Lauren swung round, trying to stay calm even though her blood was coursing through her like a competition dinghy in full sail.

'I haven't a clue,' she said huskily. 'It's probably a planet.'

'Which one?'

'I don't know.' With every cell yearning beneath her waist-fastened shirt and shorts, she shrugged and suggested, 'Venus?'

'The Roman Goddess of Beauty.' But he was looking at her, not the star, and Lauren's heart seemed to do a double somersault. 'Did you know,' he said, 'that all the features of that planet are named after women?'

Her laugh was tremulous, tense. 'No, I didn't.' She held her breath as he advanced. He was still wearing the clothes he had worn that morning, although his shoes were discarded and his unbuttoned shirt was hanging loose over his hip-hugging trousers. 'So you do know something about the universe!'

She saw the wry smile he pulled as he moved closer out of the shadows. 'Far more, I think, than I will ever know about women.'

She laughed again, the strands that had escaped

from her loosely tied hair caressing her face with the warm wind.

'We're that complex to you? And I thought you were the world's expert on the opposite sex.'

'That,' he stated meaningfully, 'is a totally erroneous conclusion arrived at by over-zealous members of the press. Well?'

'Well, what?' she parried breathlessly, knowing what he was going to ask, and wondering how he could stand there sounding so matter-of-fact when her heart was beating so ridiculously fast she thought it was going to burst.

'Do you agree we should get married?'

Just like that.

'I haven't given any thought to it,' she prevaricated, even though she had been thinking of nothing else all day. 'I hadn't realised you were serious.'

'You think I would joke about a thing like that?'

It was exactly what she had been thinking only a few moments ago, but tremulously she responded with, 'I don't know. I would have thought that you'd have at least telephoned if you'd been expecting an answer from me.'

'I am not in the habit, *cara*, of making life-changing decisions over the telephone.'

Life-changing decisions?

The mind-blowing realisation that he was deadly serious stunned Lauren into silent incredulity.

'You want to be with me, do you not?' he prompted before she had gathered her wits to say anything.

How could he doubt it?

'What do you think?' she asked him tremulously.

'I am not sure. That is why I want to hear it from your own lips,' he insisted.

'Of course I do,' she whispered, with half a glance towards the white-crested waves that were drawing dark sweeping patterns over the sand. 'But there's more to getting married than simply wanting to be with someone.'

He laughed softly. 'Is there?' And when she turned back to him with her frown questioning the seriousness of his question, 'Of course,' he agreed. 'There is mutual respect and trust and even admiration. And, on top of all that, compatibility. And there are many ways—and one in particular...' his tone had become as sultry and seductive as the tropical paradise they were standing in '...that show we are compatible, *carissima.*'

'Even though we're from different worlds?'

She heard his breath catch momentarily before he said, 'I am asking you to share mine with me, Lauren.'

So why was she hesitating? she wondered, and knew the answer without even having to think about it. She wanted him to tell her that he felt the same way she did. She desperately wanted him to tell her that he loved her.

'Why?' she stalled. 'Because you can't think of a simpler way to keep Danny with you?'

The silence was broken only by the intrusion of the sighing wind in some nearby palms.

'You are right,' he said, in a way that didn't actually convey whether he was jesting or not. 'I cannot think of a better or simpler way.' Reaching out, he traced a finger lightly down the curve of her cheek. 'I am not the...what is the phrase?... sentimental type, *mia cara.*

But will you believe me when I say that…you mean a great deal to me?'

A great deal.

Her heart leaped in her breast.

Not love.

But, as he had just said, such sentimental words weren't really in Emiliano's vocabulary.

'You mean…' more hopeful, she leaned into his hand with a little shiver of pleasure as it burned a sensual trail along her neck '…you've finally decided I'm not a gold-digger?'

He gave a low chuckle from deep in his throat. 'Would you be procrastinating over giving me your answer if you were?'

'Well…' She pretended to consider this. 'I might,' she teased, massaging her lower lip with a forefinger. She knew a sharp thrill as his lashes drooped, following the provocative little gesture.

'To what purpose?' he enquired.

'To make you believe my intentions were honourable? That I really wasn't after your money?'

'Of course.' There was a kind of self-censure in the way he spoke those two words. But then hadn't he himself suggested that her stand-off was all part of a clever feminine technique before?

'I was only joking!' she breathed, suddenly wishing she hadn't reminded him when she sensed the slight shift in his mood. 'I'm sorry. Bad joke.'

'In that case, are you going to give me your answer?'

'What do you think?' she murmured.

His hands were on her shoulders. 'Let me hear you say it.' He sounded in agony.

'Yes! Oh, yes!' she said, flinging her arms around

his neck. The next instant she was being caught against him and his mouth was desperately seeking hers.

She was his—now and for ever—and she let him know it in the only way she knew how, by giving herself up to his amazing lovemaking right there on the beach. As nature intended. With no holds barred. And only the sea and sand and a universe of wakening stars to witness their passion.

CHAPTER EIGHT

THE WHITE GAUZE of Lauren's dress was moving gently around her calves and the wind was stirring the white petals of the periwinkles she had entwined in her hair, which she had caught up at the sides, leaving the rest cascading over her shoulders.

Standing barefoot on the pink sand, under an archway decked with flowers, she couldn't help marvelling at how she and Emiliano had managed to come so far in the space of a few short weeks.

Three, to be precise.

That was how long it had been since that morning he had floored her by suggesting that they get married. And ever since that staggering moment, here on this beach, when she'd realised that he had meant it, it was as if someone had hit the fast forward button on Lauren's life.

Although they had both agreed on a small private wedding, with only a few discreet members of Emiliano's staff in attendance, there had still been a marriage licence to apply for and flowers and photographs to think about, food and drink for the buffet, as well as a honeymoon to arrange. Then there had been the things to take care of at home.

Because she and Emiliano were keeping the wedding secret from the wider world—and therefore the Press—until such time as they were ready to announce it, she had simply told her boss, when she had handed in her notice at the garden centre, that she had decided to extend her stay in the Caribbean. Likewise, Fiona, when Lauren had telephoned her, although she had been dying to reveal her happy news, especially when the woman was being good enough to come in and check on the house and pick up any post on a regular basis. Not to mention feeding the fish!

But now the big day had arrived and everything had fallen neatly into place, even the choosing of her dress, which she had decided to keep as simple as possible. That was why she had settled on a fine floaty affair that she had purchased on the island and which, with its Grecian neckline, finely layered skirt and zigzagging hemline, made her look more like an ethereal nymph from some Impressionist painter's romantic imagination, she'd thought fancifully when she'd put it on earlier, than a very eligible billionaire's bride.

Now she looked up at the tall man standing beside her, with his heart-stopping looks and a loosely tailored Italian white shirt and light trousers enhancing his superb body, and her green eyes expressed only one sentiment.

I love you.

He still hadn't said those words to her. But wasn't it evident enough, she decided, from the sparkling solitaire diamond he had placed on her finger a week ago? From the vows he was about to take? From the way he could never get enough of her—either in bed or out of it?

As the man officiating started to speak, Lauren tried to savour every second of these precious moments so that she could tell Daniele and her own children about it in years to come. Yet she felt so deliriously happy that she could only stand there as if in a dream, feeling as though it was all happening to someone else—some fairy tale bride.

Two bouquets had arrived for her that morning—white lilies from the staff and two dozen red roses from Emiliano. Consequently, she had interwoven a few of them into the wedding bouquet, which she had made up herself. The result was a beautiful blend of colourful island flowers interspersed with the roses and the lilies.

'I think you should add more of a different colour,' Constance had advised solemnly when she'd come into Lauren's room in her lovely new turquoise suit and hat and seen Lauren putting the finishing touches to the bouquet that morning. 'I don't hold much with superstition myself, but there are some folks who say too much red and white together signifies bad luck.'

'Oh, Constance! Don't be a killjoy!' Lauren had laughed, having lived far too long with her mother's superstitions ever to take anyone else's too seriously. After all, what bad luck could possibly lie in marrying the man she loved?

As they pledged their troth to each other in front of the little group who were witnessing the sealing of their bond, Lauren smiled adoringly up at Emiliano and met such an intensity of emotion mirrored in his dark eyes that her heart seemed to overflow with her love for him.

Their lingering kiss was met by cheers from everyone gathered there on the sand. When Emiliano broke the kiss at last, his eyes still held Lauren's for a long time.

Now he turned to take their nephew from a happily beaming Constance, who had been holding the little boy throughout the ceremony. Her good wishes couldn't have been warmer or more deeply meant, Lauren thought fondly, with a heartfelt smile at Emiliano's housekeeper, with whom she had grown to share the same kind of rapport as Emiliano.

'What do you think of your *mamma* and *papà* now, *piccolo*?' he asked the toddler, who was dressed in a smart little white shirt and red shorts for the occasion. He ruffled the little boy's silky hair. 'Will you not be secure and happy for the rest of your life?'

The rest of your life.

That said it all, Lauren realised, with her heart soaring now like a bird high on the currents.

'Now, everyone enjoy the food!' Emiliano advised with a jerk of his head towards the buffet and the barbecue that was already filling the air with mouthwatering aromas. His staff laughed with him as he added, 'I know that is the only reason you came!'

A steel band struck up then, hired for the occasion for their professionalism and diplomacy, adding the final touch to what was a truly tropical event.

Their wedding couldn't have been more perfect, Lauren thought, as the day wore on. Glasses chinked. Laughter and conversation filled the air, becoming more animated as the champagne flowed. A camera clicked as the only photographer who had been invited to attend captured memorable moments for eternity. The music rang out. And all against a backdrop of pink sand and waving palms, and a sun that was sinking lower above the oblivious sea.

'Happy?' Emiliano asked, looking down at her where she stood, clamped to his side, as the sky started to turn red and the sun threw a fiery mantle over the waves. It was where she had been for most of the afternoon, so that whenever he had left her—however briefly—she'd felt as though she was missing part of herself.

'Now, why on earth are you asking that, Mr Cannavaro?' she laughed, and earned herself an extra tight squeeze before his mouth descended deliciously over hers.

Their cases were packed, since they were flying off the following morning to spend a couple of days in New York. Something, Emiliano had observed, laughingly, that she sorely needed to do. 'To stock up on a new wardrobe,' he'd commented when he saw the modest amount of budget-conscious clothing she had packed in the new suitcase he had insisted on buying for her to replace the battered old case she had arrived with, and which she had had since starting her brief spell at university. They were only taking a short honeymoon as they were keen to get back for Daniele. Tonight, however, their wedding night, they were going to spend right there.

Daniele was already in bed, taken up by a lovingly crooning Constance over an hour ago.

Now, as they walked up the terrace steps with their arms around each other, Lauren knew that their special day could only get better.

They were laughing as they stepped through into the cool luxury of the house. Unaware of anything but Emiliano and that strong arm still wrapped around her, Lauren looked up on hearing him catch his breath.

A slim and chic dark-haired woman had just emerged from the salon. In a pale blue designer shift dress and matching stiletto-heeled sandals that complemented the sapphires in her ears and which also adorned her wrist and throat, Claudette looked not dissimilar from the model who had graced the covers of France's glossiest fashion magazines more than twenty-five years ago.

'*Buona sera*, Emiliano.' Her years living in Italy had made her as much a native of that country as he was. In fact Lauren recalled Emiliano saying that his father's widow still lived there, with her new husband.

'Claudette.' A note of wary surprise laced her stepson's voice. 'I gather you heard it from the paparazzo before I was able to tell you myself.' It took him only a moment to recover himself before he remembered his manners and introduced Lauren to his stepmother.

'Yes, we've met,' Claudette said dismissively, with even less warmth than she had shown Lauren at her younger stepson's wedding two years ago. 'Emiliano, can we talk?'

'Of course.' A frown was pleating his brows even as he sliced Lauren a look that from any other man she would have said expressed regret. From Emiliano it seemed to signify mild impatience.

Realising she wasn't wanted, she smiled and said, 'Of course. You go ahead. I've got a hundred and one things I need to do before we go off on our…trip tomorrow.' For some reason she couldn't explain, she avoided saying 'honeymoon' in front of Claudette.

* * *

Watching his new bride walking away, Emiliano dragged his gaze reluctantly back to his stepmother.

'Why didn't you telephone first?' It surprised him that she'd want to be here, when he'd imagined that she wouldn't care one way or the other, and yet he felt slightly irritated as he followed her back into the salon.

'And have you put me off with the lame excuse that you were keeping it entirely private?' She gave a tight little laugh.

'How did you find out?'

'Not all the trustees of your father's estate are as uncommunicative as you are, Emiliano. Or, I should say, one of the junior assistants to the trustees, otherwise he might not have let the information slip out. Anyway, the man probably thought I knew. What I hadn't realised was that it was going to happen so fast.' Her clear blue eyes viewed him interestedly as she sat down on one of the sofas. 'She isn't…'

Emiliano drew in a sharp breath. 'Whether she is or not is hardly anyone's business but ours.'

'You're right.' A shrug of a slim shoulder constituted a dismissive apology. 'Anyway, I just happened to be in Florida because Pierre's in Bermuda golfing, and I was going to fly down here to see you anyway. You know—to try and patch things up. Even before I knew about your wedding arrangements. Your brother's funeral didn't seem like an appropriate time to say all I needed to say. I was only hoping that I could get here before the actual ceremony.'

'I am sorry you missed it.'

He wasn't sure he meant that. Apart from Angelo's funeral, when he and Claudette had exchanged only mutual condolences, Emiliano hadn't spoken to her since he had flown over to see her in Milan over four months ago. They had argued, as they always had, when, worried about his brother, he had accused her of condoning Angelo's over-indulgence in everything from booze to gambling to women. He had also accused her of not being interested enough in her grandson even to try and find out from Angelo where he was. He regretted it now, but he had been angry with her indifference to the whole situation. He had been made even angrier when she had pointed out that Daniele was only her *step*-grandson and therefore not her responsibility, but Angelo's.

'Is that all you care about?' he remembered saying savagely. 'Whose responsibility he is?'

Claudette had turned defensive and said, 'Don't have a go at me. It's your brother you need to be talking to.'

He gave himself a censuring mental shake. He didn't want to think about any of that now.

'I'm sorry I have to bring you unexpectedly bad news,' the woman expressed, looking up at him now with something remarkably like sincerity in her coldly beautiful face. 'Especially on the day that is supposed to be the happiest of your life. Or is that only for a woman?' Another humourless laugh from her this time made her sound tense and strained.

'Claudette, what is it?' Emiliano felt his patience waning. Claudette had always affected him like this, he thought regretfully, wishing he could have enjoyed the same harmonious rapport with her that his brother had. 'Is there some problem back home? With your finances? Are you having difficulty in securing your allowance from my father's estate?'

She looked at him long and hard. So long and hard it was almost unnerving, he thought, with a self-effacing grimace, because whatever problem he had ever had to face in his life—or would be likely to face—there never had been—or would be—one that he couldn't solve.

'Emiliano...' Claudette's tone was tentative, almost nervous '...I think you had better sit down.'

When Lauren opened the door of the master suite, for a moment she couldn't believe her eyes.

Constance and some of the staff had been busy putting their own personal touches to the celebrations. The huge bed had been turned back with a hand-embroidered silk throw over a white satin coverlet, with matching pillowcases over the plump pillows, to which they had added a host of cushions in luxuriously padded and embroidered white satin. The brass spindles of the bedstead had been decorated too, intertwined somehow with the pink and yellow and red trumpets of freshly picked hibiscus flowers.

A hand-sculpted vase of some exotic white blooms she couldn't even name stood on the low chest beneath one of the windows, their heady scent intoxicating on the air.

Nature, too, had lent a hand with a slice of new moon peeping above the ferny foliage of a jacaranda tree just beyond the window. The lizards and tree frogs had already begun their evening chorus, their shrill whistling an accompaniment for the steel band that was still beating out its reggae rhythm for the few revellers who had stayed to linger on the beach.

Their cases stood in the dressing room adjacent to the en suite bathroom, waiting to be put into the car the following day.

Slipping off her dress and putting it carefully away in one of the floor to ceiling wardrobes, Lauren took a shower. Afterwards, creaming her body with a luxurious lotion from one of the frosted glass dispensers that had discreetly appeared in Emiliano's bathroom since she had moved into his room, she began to wonder where he was.

Claudette and he must have a lot of catching up to do, she realised, aware that he hadn't seen his stepmother in happy circumstances for some months; knowing that they hadn't always got on.

Still, it was good of her to take the time to come and see her stepson on his wedding day, she mused, even if Claudette had clearly not taken to his new wife, any more than she had taken to Vikki when she had married his brother.

Slipping on a green silk robe, her body pulsing with excited anticipation, she went through into the dressing room to brush her hair.

A prominent red star hung parallel with the centre of the open window. She wondered what it was, and in a flight of fancy wondered what her mother would have made of it—called it. The North Star? No. Wrong hemisphere, surely? Or perhaps it was part of the Taurus constellation, in which case her mother would probably have said it was the vivid red eye of the angry bull.

In front of one of the long mirrors she started brushing her hair, and then, in a deliciously abandoned moment, swept it up above her head. Her own eyes were bright with anticipation, she noticed, and the upper curves of her breasts were clearly visible beneath the gaping 'V' of her green robe. Exactly the same emerald-green that she had been wearing the night she had met Emilano, she realised, her heart giving an excited little leap when she heard the bedroom door handle suddenly being turned.

He was closing the door behind him. She could see his reflection clearly in the mirror, where she was still standing with her hair pushed up in that provocative way and an unintentionally provocative smile playing around her mouth. But then she wanted him to see her just as she saw herself at that moment. Wanton and alluring. Naked beneath her robe. A woman eager to please the man she was madly in love with and had promised to cherish for eternity.

Or a woman...cruelly, she heard her sister's voice mentally mocking her, even though she tried to blank it out...*a woman who's just landed the catch of the century!*

'I thought you'd changed your mind about joining me,' she purred softly at his reflection, bringing her tongue unconsciously across her top lip. 'I was getting ready to send out a search party,' she teased. 'Or to check to see if you'd forgotten which room I was in.'

She spoke with all the love and warmth and tenderness oozing from her towards this man who, even with his back to her, still managed to look as though he'd been put on this earth purely to please womankind. And yet he was hers—and only hers, she thought blissfully, until the end of time.

But then he turned round, and even in the mirror

she could see the cold, hard angles of his unsmiling features.

'What is it?' she whispered, whipping round, her spirits tumbling like the flaming red hair about her shoulders as she came out of the dressing room. 'What's wrong?'

CHAPTER NINE

'WHY DID YOU not tell me that Daniele is not my brother's child?'

His question hit Lauren like a thunderbolt through solid steel.

'What are you talking about?' she queried, with her throat contracting.

'The fact that your sister was pregnant with another man's child when she married my brother, and that you knew about it!'

The colour leeched out of Lauren's face, and for those few moments when she couldn't speak she saw hard grooves deepening around Emiliano's mouth.

'So you did know.' His voice was barely a whisper.

'No.' She was shaking her head, her answer little more than a croak.

'Are you saying she didn't tell you?' Harsh scepticism ran through every word.

'No!' It was an adamantly voiced denial. 'I mean…'

'Yes?' he prompted, like a cold, remorseless interrogator and not the man who had made those vows to her so sincerely and apparently lovingly just a few hours ago.

'I mean that when Vikki left Angelo she…she told

me she had said some awful things to him. She said he'd been threatening to hang on to Danny to stop her leaving so, in order to get away from him, *and* keep her baby, she told him she'd had an affair the last time they'd broken up and that Danny wasn't his.'

Lauren remembered how shocked she had been on hearing that; remembered the relief she had felt when her sister had shown distinct remorse for saying it.

'She apologised to him afterwards.' During one of their mutually antagonising telephone conversations, Lauren suspected. 'Made it clear to him that she'd only said it because he was being so difficult.'

'And because she realised she stood to lose a nice fat maintenance settlement if she didn't.'

'That's not true!' Her sister had done a lot of questionable things in her time, but she would never have lied about her baby's paternity for the sake of her own ends, would she? 'Has your stepmother just told you all this?' she demanded, hating the doubts that were seeping through her with regard to Vikki's motives, yet unable to forget her sister's parting words that last day when she had left Danny in Lauren's temporary— or, as it turned out—permanent care.

I'm going to screw him for every penny I can get!

'Why?' she queried with her eyes narrowing when Emiliano didn't respond. 'To try and ruin your wedding day? Doesn't she want you to be happy?'

He made a hard, deprecating sound down his nostrils. 'Claudette and I might not always have got along, but my stepmother is not deliberately vindictive,' he informed her coldly. 'She had the facts directly from Angelo himself just a couple of weeks before he died.'

'So why didn't she tell you then? Why didn't he?' she persisted, desperate for some answers.

'We weren't in contact.' He wasn't spelling it out in so many words, but Lauren guessed he was referring to both Claudette and his brother. 'Aside from which, I was the last person in whom my brother would have confided,' he stated grimly. 'More to the point, Lauren, why didn't *you*?'

'Because it didn't even cross my mind! And if it had, I really wouldn't have thought it was worth mentioning,' she uttered, flabbergasted. 'Vikki and Angelo...' She couldn't even say: *have gone*. 'It was just something Vikki said so she wouldn't lose custody of Danny, but she regretted saying it.'

'And you want to make me think you were really naïve enough to believe that?'

His remark hurt. Not least because in questioning her sister's scruples he was also questioning hers, just as he had done in the past. Only this time it was a thousand times worse because she loved him; because she was wearing his wedding ring on her finger.

'How can you say that?' It was hard containing the emotion in her voice when his accusations and suspicions were making a mockery of everything in a room designed for a night of loving. 'Let alone even imagine that I would have let you think...' She shook her head to try and clear it. 'Of course Danny's Angelo's! A *Cannavaro*,' she stressed, refusing to harbour any doubts in her mind. 'OK. He looks more like my side of the family than yours, but he does have some Cannavaro characteristics. You even commented on it once or twice yourself!'

'A man can convince himself of anything if he wants to,' he assured her dismissively.

'And you obviously want to!' she snapped back, wondering why he was refusing to budge or even give an inch. 'So what are you trying to say? That I lied to you to get you to marry me?'

'Only you know the answer to that, Lauren.'

She gazed up into his harsh, judgemental features, her own face lined with pain and incredulity as she whispered, 'What are you saying?'

She could feel herself trembling as he took a folded piece of paper from his trouser pocket and opened it out.

'Perhaps you'd care to explain this.'

He didn't show it to her, just began quoting from the text of what Lauren realised, in shocked amazement, was a letter she had written to Vikki shortly after her sister had walked out on his brother.

'"*You can't go on living with Matthew like you did when you and Angelo broke up before. It's not being fair to him now you're married, and you're never going to make Angelo believe Daniele's his if he finds out.*"'

'Where did you get that?'

As she tried to snatch it from him, Emiliano continued remorselessly. '"*If he does, you'll lose everything. Daniele* will lose everything...*"*'

'I meant his *family*!' Lauren riposted emphatically. She had written that letter to try to get Vikki to stop making things difficult for herself, as well as to apologise to Angelo, when her sister had seemed too proud and reluctant at first to contact him. 'Where did you get it?' she demanded, with her nostrils flaring as she watched Emiliano toss the letter down on the bridal bed in a disgusted gesture that sent darts of pain and anguish spearing through her.

'My brother found it among your sister's things, which the police had taken to their marital home at the time of the accident, and which he discovered when he was well enough to go through them afterwards.'

Things that Lauren hadn't been allowed to take as Angelo had still been legally Vikki's next of kin.

'You told me you hadn't seen her for years until shortly before their wedding.'

'I hadn't!'

'So how did you know she had been shacking up with this Matthew before?'

'She told me!' Wings of angry colour were spreading across her cheeks. 'And she wasn't shacking up with him! Matthew was just a friend.'

'A very good one, apparently!'

Good enough to put Vikki up in his London flat whenever she'd burnt her bridges. To love her as he had since they'd been teenagers in Cumbria, when her sister didn't even fancy him and only ever wanted to use him as a stopgap. Someone to shoulder her troubles— as someone always had, Lauren remembered unhappily—when her sister couldn't cope with the problems she'd often made for herself.

It was clear, though, that telling Emiliano that would scarcely help to exonerate her in her supposed conspiracy with her sister. And who was to say that Vikki hadn't, in one of her capricious moments, been persuaded into letting Matthew take her to bed at some stage just for the hell of it? Or even some other man, for that matter?

If your brother didn't think Daniele was his, and

that I knew about it, why didn't he confront me with it? she nearly asked through her mounting doubts about her sister, but then decided it was totally unnecessary. Hadn't Angelo Cannavaro's actions said it all in the way he had simply abandoned his son after Vikki died? And yet why had he taken so long to show that letter to his stepmother? Hadn't he wanted to accept that he might just have driven his wife into the arms of another man?

Now, though, looking up into his brother's satanically dark features, she noticed for the first time how strained he looked. *Devastated* was the word that sprang to Lauren's mind.

Yet he couldn't feel half as devastated as she did right at that moment, knowing what he thought about her. It didn't help in any way to realise how incriminating that letter sounded, how guilty it made her seem.

'You can't really believe all this. Unless you've got so little trust in me that you think I could be guilty of all the things you're accusing me of. In which case, why did you marry me? Unless…'

'Unless what?' he enquired coldly.

'Unless you had some ulterior motive.' After all, he had never once said that he loved her.

His eyes narrowed into slits as he tilted his head to look at her. 'Like what?'

'Daniele.'

He gave a harsh bark of laughter. 'Is that what you think?'

'Why not? You can hardly think very much of me if you can accuse me of trying to trick you even before we've had our honeymoon.'

'I haven't accused you of trying to trick me.'

'Haven't you?'

This time he didn't answer, and it was obvious why. He still thought she had been party to a gross deception by Vikki and had carried on that deception.

'If you loved me you wouldn't have questioned my honesty,' she said, tortured by the fact that he had. 'But you've never really stopped believing I wanted you for what you could give me, have you? You've always judged me on something you believe I've said or written, without even bothering to look beyond it. You just put two and two together and come up with sixteen! But if you think as little of me as that, then it has to be true what I said. That you married me for the simple reason I mentioned just now: Danny. You wanted him back where he belongs. Belonged,' she corrected, hurting, unable to believe that all this was happening—that it was being said. 'And you took the best possible route you could think of to make sure you got him. After all, in marrying me you weren't only getting custody of your nephew... Correction. What you *thought* was your nephew,' she inserted pointedly, 'but a ready-made mother to look after him as well!'

Not to mention a guaranteed willing bed partner, she thought wretchedly, although she couldn't bring herself to tell him that.

'If you imagine that, then we should both be examining our motives,' he said heavily.

'Perhaps we should!' she retorted, wishing she wasn't being driven to saying things like this, unable to believe they were having their first row with their marriage ceremony barely over.

But it was more than a row, wasn't it? she thought achingly. He was questioning her honesty. Her integrity. Her morals. Everything. Everything, in fact, that made her who she was.

His lashes came down as though he was tired suddenly. Tired of arguing. Tired of what, for him, at least, must have been a long, pointless charade.

'What are you thinking?' Lauren asked quietly, not wanting to be affected by those incredibly charismatic features, the proud sweep of his forehead, that bump in his nose, that shadowed jaw and that cruelly sensuous mouth that had imparadised her on so many occasions, but she was.

'I am not thinking anything right now.' Hands in his pockets, he moved past her to stand looking out of one of the bedroom windows. The music had ceased. The band was packing up. Even the last of the buffet was being cleared away. 'I don't know what to think,' he said.

'Well, I do.' She lifted her shoulder in a hopeless little gesture, trying to stem the tears she was determined to contain. She couldn't believe how calm she sounded, how very much in control of herself, as she told him, 'I don't think I want to be sharing a bed with you tonight.'

He swung round and looked at her for a long moment.

His eyes were resting on the soft heart of her face with its velvety red brows, green eyes and that slightly turned up nose with its dusting of freckles as though he wanted to consign it to his memory. Then, with a slide of his gaze to her provocatively parted robe, that even now made her pulses throb traitorously in response, he gave the briefest nod of acknowledgement before walking away, out of the room.

* * *

Lauren hadn't slept a wink.

The sofa in the dressing room hadn't been designed for sleeping on, but she hadn't been able to bring herself to use the bed that had been prepared for a first night of conjugal bliss. Neither had she wanted to risk setting tongues wagging amongst the staff by creeping back to her old room, where she had dressed so happily for her wedding less than twenty-four hours before.

Now, with the first light of dawn peeping through the blind, she eased herself up and found that she was aching mentally and physically from that dreadful scene with him the night before as she brought herself gingerly into the bedroom.

He hadn't come back. Not that she had really expected him to. The room was as they had left it and the big bed hadn't been slept in. The hibiscus flowers woven through the brass spindles had dropped, designed only to last a day.

Like her marriage, she thought excruciatingly, and wondered, as she had been doing throughout the long night, where on earth they could go from here.

He had said that relationships were built on trust, but he had never actually stopped doubting her. He had never trusted her, had he? she realised, agonised. How could he have, she reasoned, if just one thoughtlessly worded letter—and it had been thoughtless, she accepted, stupidly so—could resurrect his past opinion of her and nullify everything they had between them? Or what she had imagined they had had, she thought, torturously. But she couldn't begin life with a man who clearly despised her. Nor did she want to, she realised, choking back tears, as she had been doing for most of the night. Any more than he wanted to be with her. And even if Vikki hadn't cheated on Angelo and Daniele *was* his son, Emiliano would never believe now that the toddler was a Cannavaro, which gave him no claim to her little nephew, or left him even wanting one. But it was his lack of trust in her that was hardest to bear. So where did that leave her and Emiliano?

Painfully, she acknowledged the answer she had been refusing to acknowledge all night.

Absolutely nowhere.

Now, on legs that felt as heavy as lead, she began moving around the room, unlocking her new suitcase, pulling on clothes, doing the things she knew she had to do, no matter how painful it might be, knowing there was only one possible course of action she could take.

CHAPTER TEN

THE MIST WAS closing in over the Cumbrian hillsides, bringing with it the fine rain that had been threatening all day.

'Are you sure you're all right?' Fiona asked Lauren, who was standing by the table in the farmhouse kitchen, spooning some softly boiled egg into Daniele's mouth. 'I know you've come back home to some miserable weather, but since you've been back you don't seem to have been yourself. You're dark under the eyes—which tells me you're not sleeping properly—and I'd say you were looking rather off-colour, despite that wonderful Caribbean tan!' She sent a mock stern glance towards the high chair. 'Has this little rascal been keeping you awake all hours?'

'No,' Lauren said swiftly, not wishing to implicate Danny as the reason for her misery.

'What then?' Folding a tea towel, the woman looked solemnly down her nose at Lauren. 'It hasn't got anything to do with that delicious-looking hunk who whisked you off at a moment's notice, has it? Has he been making you promises that he couldn't deliver?'

'No, of course not,' Lauren lied, thinking how near the mark Fiona's observation was. She hated not telling the truth, but she was unable to share the events of the past few weeks with anyone, however kind they might be. Also, she wasn't wearing Emiliano's rings. She had left them on the cabinet beside the bed that had never been part of her married life, and she was only glad that she had agreed with him to keep their wedding secret from everyone but those who had needed to know, so that she wouldn't now have to face the shame and humiliation of telling anyone that it had all been a terrible mistake. 'I'm fine,' she emphasised, sending her obviously concerned friend a falsely bright smile. 'I've just had a lot to think about after being away for so long, that's all,' she added, cutting a piece of brown toast into strips for Daniele to dip into his egg.

'Soldiers', her mother used to call them.

Suddenly she had such a yearning to sob her heart out on those gentle maternal shoulders that she had to pull her own shoulders back under the chunky sweater she was wearing over her jeans to stop herself falling apart in front of Fiona.

'I really am fine,' she reiterated, managing a more convincing smile for the woman who was shrugging into her large cape of a raincoat. 'Thanks for locking up. I'll see you tomorrow.'

'You can count on it.' The woman knew better than to ferret information out of her if she didn't want to give it, Lauren thought, even though she knew she hadn't managed to fool Fiona.

'Drive carefully,' Lauren called after her, already rebuking herself for anticipating the relief of being alone. But how could she have told the stalwart Fiona that she had fallen in love with and married the so-called 'delicious-looking hunk', and that her marriage had ended even before it had begun? She couldn't, any more than she could have told Constance why she had been taking off alone with Danny five days ago, leaving before Emiliano had even returned.

She had managed to hold back her tears until she had climbed into the taxi. But it was while she had been travelling down the drive, away from the house where she had been so happy, and seen the housekeeper standing there on the steps with her features clearly in turmoil that it had all proved too much to bear.

Had Emiliano telephoned her that day after he had discovered she'd left, she could never have handled speaking to him, Lauren thought achingly, and she had kept her cell phone switched off for the whole of that day and for the rest of that weekend. From the moment she had switched it back on, her heart had started pounding whenever it began to ring. It was with mixed emotions that she answered those calls, only to discover that it wasn't him.

Well, what could he say?

Let's get Daniele tested. Then I can decide whether you've been telling me the truth or not.

If that was what it was going to take, then she didn't want him like that.

It had been fairly easy getting a local company with a six-seater plane to get her off the island, where she had picked up a flight to the UK from one of the larger islands.

It had been an endlessly long and bumpy ride home, especially at the outset, with storms starting to brew up over the Caribbean. During the flight she heard one of the cabin crew telling another that several of the major islands in the area had closed their runways to any further air traffic. It was with immense and yet agonising relief that she knew she was lucky to have managed to get away when she had. In a moment of wild imaginings she'd realised that if her plane went down, taking her and Danny with it, Emiliano would have been a widower. With a pain lodging in her chest that had refused to go away, she'd wondered if he would even have cared.

Now Lauren heard Fiona saying something as she was letting herself out of the house, but she had been too deep in her anguished thoughts to catch what it was. It wasn't until Brutus trotted in—as he often did when he was out on one of his walks and found her back door open—that Lauren realised the woman had been talking to the dog.

'Come on, darling,' she said to Daniele, dipping one of his 'soldiers' into his egg. He was more interested, though, in the dog that had sunk into its favourite spot near the Aga so that he missed the spoon altogether and wound up with a bright yellow smear on his cheek.

Rushing to get some kitchen roll, Lauren's heart went out to him.

Through no fault of his own, he'd been responsible for bringing about two Cannavaro marriages, she realised torturously, under no illusion that that was the main reason Emiliano had proposed.

As for his brother...

He probably wouldn't even have considered getting married if Vikki hadn't deceived him by conceiving Daniele in the first place, which meant that the little boy had had a Cannavaro man abandon him not once, but twice, she thought, aching for him—just cast him aside as if he were no more than a pawn in a game of chess.

She couldn't cry. She *wouldn't!*

Tomorrow, she promised herself, she would pop down to the garden centre to try and get her old job back. If they'd still have her. And then, at some stage in the near future, she would take steps to see how she could go about changing Daniele's family name to hers.

As Emiliano came silently into the farmhouse kitchen, the domestic scene that met him tugged at something way down deep inside him.

Lauren was leaning with her back to him over the high chair, wiping something diligently off her nephew's face. The dog they had rescued, and which had trotted inside when her horsey friend had let him in, was lying on an old blanket in front of the Aga, while the illustrious trio…he remembered how shamelessly he had teased her about her fish…were swimming contentedly in a little oblong tank on the dresser. He wondered why he hadn't even noticed them before.

'Da. Da,' said the toddler, pushing Lauren's hand away. His broad grin at Emiliano sent a shaft of emotion through the man's long lean frame.

Lauren swung round, catching her breath as she saw who it was her nephew was smiling at. Her legs felt as though they were going to buckle under her and she grasped the edge of the table for support.

'Emiliano…'

'Da!' Daniele said triumphantly.

'No, he's not your Da, Danny.' She wasn't looking at her nephew, only at the heart-stopping figure of the man standing in the doorway. Raindrops were clinging to his thick dark hair and there were several damp spots on the front of his shirt beneath his dark suit jacket.

'Hello, Lauren,' he greeted her, more calmly than she could imagine herself feeling ever again.

'Wh-what are you doing here?'

'Looking for you.' His voice was toneless above the quiet hum of the fridge.

'Why?' She could scarcely speak from the speed at which her heart was beating.

'I believe we're still married,' he said softly, moving away from the door.

'For what it's worth.' Dear heaven! Don't crack up now! she prayed, as emotion welled up in her. Determinedly, though, she forced her shoulders back and, lifting her small chin, added, 'Which, in your opinion, amounted to very little.'

He gave an almost indiscernible nod and his lashes came down as though in acknowledgement of what she was saying before he put a small parcel he had been carrying down on a worktop.

'Da. *Da.*' Daniele was straining to get out of his high chair, vying for his attention.

'Anyway, don't worry. It's a situation that can be easily rectified,' Lauren steeled herself to say.

'Because it hasn't been consummated?' he suggested, with his mouth pulling down at one corner. He was moving over to the straining toddler.

'Don't touch him!' Her swift command stopped him in his tracks, the fingers that had been reaching out to her nephew's cheek suspended in mid-air. 'You have no right.'

He gave another almost imperceptible nod, and let his arm fall. 'I guess I deserved that,' he said, his breath coming unevenly now.

'So why are you here?'

He sent a half-cocked smile to the little boy whose arm was outstretched in its little denim sleeve and whose face crumpled as he strained complainingly towards him.

'I need…want you to come back with me,' he stated, seeming to change course part-way through his mind-blowing statement.

'Why?' she enquired poignantly again. 'So we can pretend to be the happily wedded couple people are imagining we are until—'

'Until what?' he enquired almost dispassionately.

'Until you decide a suitable enough time has elapsed for us to go our separate ways? So you don't have to lose face or do any awkward explaining to your staff or whoever else might have known we were getting married? Isn't that the sort of thing people from your world do?'

She thought he was going to say something in response to her derogatory remark about his world, but all he said was, '*Will* you come back with me?'

If that's what you want!

Her heart ached to say it. To grasp a few more months or weeks with him—however short—to try and change his totally wrong and hurtful opinion of her. But there were such things as dignity and self-respect. Danny's as well as hers.

'You mean be prepared to ignore the fact that you called me scheming and a liar? Again.'

Once more his lashes drooped, thick ebony against

the surprisingly dark circles under his amazing eyes. 'I do not recall using either of those words to you.'

'You didn't have to!' It was almost a wail, like a tortured animal in pain.

'And I suppose it would not make a scrap of difference to you if I were to apologise.'

'And climb down from that high, superior perch?' She uttered a tremulous little laugh. 'I don't think so, Emiliano.'

His hair fell forward as he dipped his head, and Lauren wasn't sure whether it was in acknowledgement of the fact that he had been at fault or because a climb down simply wasn't in his proud Latin nature.

'And you are wrong. I do not care about saving face,' he assured her.

The hair piled loosely on top of her head quivered as she viewed him obliquely. 'What do you care about, then?' She turned her attention to Daniele, who was getting more and more restless.

'The fact that my bride of less than twenty-four hours, whom I obviously drove away, might possibly be pregnant,' he said.

She looked at him, startled, as she attempted to lift Daniele from his chair. He had grown heavier since all that healthy living in Emiliano's home, and she was finding him quite a handful to lift nowadays.

'What makes you say that?' she queried warily.

'Putting two and two together and coming up with sixteen.'

With one easy movement he swung the toddler up out of his chair, leaving Lauren reeling from the accidental brush of his hand against hers as he cooed a few soft phrases to Daniele in Italian, making him laugh, before handing him back to Lauren.

'We made love for the past three weeks without taking any precautions,' he reminded her cruelly.

In fact, from the moment she'd accepted his proposal she'd given herself to him—body and soul, Lauren thought, hurting unbelievably as she recalled their first uninhibited lovemaking on that night-shrouded beach and every wild, abandoned moment until their wedding day.

'If my wife *is* pregnant, then I want to know about it,' he stressed resolutely.

Of course. A Cannavaro heir. That was all he was interested in. All he had ever been interested in. Preserving the bloodline. His lineage. His proud and influential family name.

'If I was pregnant, do you really think I'd be stupid enough to tell you?' she retaliated, balancing Daniele on her hip. He was still wriggling, struggling to reach Emiliano, his little starfish fingers reaching out for the man to pick him up again. The man who had rejected him, and his aunt with him, when he'd decided there were no ties to bind him with either her or the little boy.

'I am afraid that even you could not hide the evidence of my child growing inside you. And I am afraid, *mia cara*...' strangely, his voice seemed to crack on that endearment '...I intend to stick around until I find out.'

'And what would you propose to do when it was born?' Lauren challenged, with emotion almost clogging her throat. 'Sue for custody now you've got the licence to be able to do it far more easily? Take it away from me like you were going to do with Danny? Well, for your information, I'm not pregnant, Emiliano. I've had my period so there isn't going to be any baby! Or anything else you can take away from me ever again!'

She started to sob, as she had done so stupidly two days ago when she'd realised that she wasn't expecting his baby. Not that she had really wanted to be. Not like this, but in happier circumstances, when her hopes and dreams had included a little brother or sister for Danny. But now those circumstances had gone, and with them her hopes and dreams, as well as any chance of ever carrying Emiliano Cannavaro's child.

Now that she had started to sob, she wasn't able to stop and, helplessly, she felt her little nephew being lifted out of her arms.

With her shoulders slumping, she turned away, her hands clamped over her face against the shaming, humiliating tears.

After a moment she heard the sound of paper rustling and then Emiliano speaking in low, dulcet tones and realised that he was speaking to Daniele.

'*Carissima…*' His voice coming from behind her now was enticingly caressing, and the hands that were suddenly resting on her shoulders were strong and sure, their warmth penetrating even through her thick sweater. 'Why are you crying?'

Because I love you! Loved you! But you're too insensitive and prejudiced to be able to see it!

'Because I want you to leave me alone. I want you to go,' she told him in a muffled voice instead, groping blindly for the tissue she'd tucked up her sleeve.

'And that is why you are weeping like this?' Gently, he turned her around, bringing her hands down to expose her tear-streaked face to his relentless gaze. 'Not because I hurt you?'

Dear God, how could he be so cruel?

'How could you hurt me?' she argued, grabbing the folded handkerchief he had taken out of his trouser pocket when she'd failed to extract her tissue and blowing her nose with it. It smelled of sunshine and warm sand and his own evocative scent. 'How could you possibly hurt someone like me?' Her words were raw, biting and sarcastic, and yet when her wet green eyes met his she recognised such an intensity of emotion in their dark depths that it almost stole her breath away. 'I'm selfish, deceitful and thoughtless! And I make lists of rich men to target—'

His mouth descending over hers silenced anything else she had been going to say. His jaw rasped against hers where he hadn't shaved for some hours, yet her lungs were filled with the achingly familiar scent of his aftershave lotion. His mouth was warm and insistent, and crazily she was responding to it, pressing her body against his and clinging to his hard strength with all her dignity and self-respect in tatters.

'No, you are not.' Emotion thickened the words he breathed against her ear. 'I am the selfish, thoughtless and undeserving one. You have taught me nothing but love and trust and affection and I did not recognise it for what it was until you had gone. I spent our wedding night driving round the island, tramping across beaches and winding up in some cheap hotel for what was left of the night when I couldn't drive or pace or think myself crazy any more. I slept late, till just gone lunchtime, and then drove like a madman to get back to you. I don't know how many speed limits I broke, but when I got back to the house and Constance told me you'd gone off in a taxi with Daniele and that old battered suitcase, I nearly went out of my mind.

'I tried telephoning you all that day and night and the day after, but I kept getting the same message: that you were unable to take my call. I knew you had shut me out deliberately and that I deserved it, and I decided that perhaps it was for the best: that I couldn't say all I needed to say to you over the phone. I decided simply to follow you, but my pilots refused to fly anywhere because of the storms, which left me stranded—unable to reach you. You were gone five days and it seemed more like five years! I have had a lot of time to mull over my mistakes, *carissima*, and being unable to do anything to make it up to you immediately was almost more than I could bear.

'I know it was not Claudette's intention to do anything to deliberately hurt me. That she only had my interests at heart. But when she showed me that letter and told me all that Angelo had told her, I know I reacted badly but it was the shock of realising—thinking that all I believed in—had put my trust in—had suddenly been taken away. Like you, I have no one left. No birth family. Only Danny. The only good thing in this world my brother left me. And the crushing knowledge that he was not even my brother's, but some other man's—some total stranger's child—was devastating enough. But then to find out and let myself believe that you knew about it and hadn't even told me. That, as a result of that, I had lost you too…' His voice was raw with the agonising emotion he couldn't express in words. 'I was so hurt—angry—devastated—and I know I said some unforgivable things to you. But when

I had walked off my initial anger and shock and started to rationalise, I accepted…no, *knew*,' he amended with a sudden tenderness in his voice, 'that you could never hurt or deceive anyone like that. And you are right.' He made a kind of self-censuring sound down his nostrils. 'I do have a grossly impossible habit of putting two and two together and arriving at sixteen, but only where you are concerned, Lauren, and there is only one reason for that.

'I love you, *carissima*. I love you more than I have ever loved anyone or anything in my life. And I know I should have told you before this, but I am telling you now. And I intend to keep saying it until I manage to convince you. Say it is at least possible. Tell me, *mia amore*.'

She couldn't believe the degree of torment she saw in the sculpted angles of his face.

'I don't—I can't—' she faltered, choking back tears of a different kind now, hardly able to grasp that he was telling her all this. Emiliano Cannavaro, who was proud and strong and so invincible, baring his soul to her as he had never done before. And as the lines scoring his wonderful and so beloved face deepened, 'I believe you,' she whispered, with her eyes glistening.

'Then will you come back with me now? Today? I will understand if you say you need time. Or even if you just want to tell me to go to hell and say it is not possible.'

'Of course I'll come back with you,' Lauren stressed, smiling, running a loving hand along his cheek. 'Only…'

'Only what?' Concern etched his features as he held

her far enough away from him to see the sudden anxiety clouding her eyes.

'What about Danny?' She glanced down at her nephew, sitting on the tattered rug where Emiliano had placed him. He was chattering to the fluffy blue pelican that the man had brought him, with the Border Collie looking interestedly on.

'And Danny too.' His gaze had followed hers to the endearing little scene in front of the Aga and, from the smile that played around his mouth and the way his dark eyes softened, there was suddenly no doubt in Lauren's mind of just how much he cared for the little boy. 'I don't care who his father is—*was*. I will love him like he is my own because he makes it impossible for me not to,' he promised, turning back to her. 'And because he has your genes—and because there is not a part of you that it is not possible to love.'

'Oh, Emiliano…' It was beyond anything she could even have dreamed of just an hour ago, and she looked up at him with love in her eyes and her heart too full to say anything except, 'I love you.'

As they kissed again Lauren wished that they could have been spared the anguish that Claudette had caused them both by her visit. But perhaps it had all happened for a reason. Emiliano was taking her and Daniele unconditionally, and she might never have realised just how much he loved her if it hadn't happened.

'We will be a family,' he pledged. 'A real family. And Danny will have brothers and sisters so that he will not be an only child for very long.'

'Hey, steady on!' Lauren laughed. 'I won't mind three or four. But you'll have to consult the stars if you're planning on more!'

'I think they will leave the decision to chance when they realise how often I will be making love to you,' he advised, with his eyes gleaming wickedly.

Then a sudden loud splash had them bursting out laughing as one of the fish did a backward flip in the tank on the dresser.

EPILOGUE

EXCITED BARKING AND childish laughter brought Lauren over to the casement window to see the five-year-old Daniele chasing his two-year-old sister, Francesca, and their two cocker spaniels around the lawn.

The red-haired little girl had been born just two weeks after Lauren and Emiliano's first wedding anniversary, and Lauren couldn't hide her smile as she watched her children running rings around their father. Literally! And Emiliano's wish for siblings for Daniele was being granted yet again, with the anticipated arrival in a few weeks' time of a new baby boy.

It had been a joint decision between her and Emiliano to give their children an English education. With that in mind, and with his American company established and running successfully now, they had decided to keep the Caribbean house purely as a tropical retreat and make their main home in England, which was why they had recently snapped up this lovely modern mansion with its sprawling grounds for children and animals alike to play in, close enough to London for Emiliano to conduct his business, and yet far enough away to enjoy the countryside too.

Space and fresh air had been a priority for Lauren, having spent so much of her life in the Lake District. She had sold the farmhouse eighteen months ago to Fiona and her new horse-trainer husband who had given the place a well-needed facelift and turned the stables and land into a thriving stud farm.

Claudette they had seen only when circumstances had demanded it during the past three years. If the woman didn't want to spend any time with her and Emiliano and the little boy they had legally adopted, then it was her loss, Lauren thought resignedly, tearing herself away from the sunny scene beyond the open window to return to sorting through the last boxes they needed to clear out of the room she had chosen for their new baby.

With just a few items left for her '*Consider*', '*Keep*' or '*Get rid of*' piles, she picked up something which, when she looked at it, seemed to suck the breath right out of her lungs.

The next instant she was racing downstairs and out into the garden as fast as her condition would allow.

'Happy birthday, Mummy!' Daniele burst out, with his baby sister like an echo just a note or two behind him, so that for a few moments Lauren had to forget what she had come out here to do as she stooped to let Daniele place the daisy chain around her neck.

'Oh, darlings, thank you!' She caught them both to her, hugging them fiercely, before they scampered off, whooping for joy.

They were as happy as any loving family could be. Probably more so, she decided, and thought, as she sometimes did, that although she had foregone a career to become a mother it had all been worth it, because she couldn't imagine ever being happier than she was right at this moment with her beautiful children and the man she loved by her side.

'You looked flushed. Are you all right?' Emiliano asked, concerned.

'I'm fine,' she reassured him, with her heart bursting with love for this man who showed so much love for her, for them all in equal measure. She only wished that the happiness her children were enjoying, and which she had enjoyed in her own childhood, he could have known just a little of in his. 'I really am fine,' she reiterated in case he was in any doubt. 'But you asked me to let you see anything I might think was important.'

He was looking down at what she had handed him, staring at it with a deepening groove between his thick black brows, but then he turned away so that she couldn't see his face.

'I found it in that box. You know, the one marked "photographs" that you've never had time to sort through.' Or perhaps he just hadn't been able to bring himself to do it, she accepted silently.

'It seems your brother did leave you something,' she whispered, knowing from the steeling of her husband's broad back beneath his casual shirt that he was dealing privately with his emotion. 'Vikki must have consented to that DNA test being done...' *hoping, or even* knowing *that it wouldn't show Daniele as anyone else's;* secretly, Lauren still wanted to believe that of her sister '...only that result came through less than a week after she died.'

'So why did Angelo disown him? And so blatantly in front of Claudette when all the time he had this...' Emiliano punched the piece of paper he was holding, his words thickened by angry disbelief.

'Perhaps he just couldn't face the responsibility of being a father when she started putting pressure on him to act like one,' Lauren suggested, the gentle understanding in her voice finally bringing him round.

He could have taken steps to prove conclusively whether or not Daniele was his brother's, but he had chosen not to, she thought, with the words he uttered next reminding her why.

'You know it would never have made a scrap of difference. It has never made a difference,' he said hoarsely, glancing towards the little boy stroking one of the dogs and whom he now knew was as much a part of him as he was of Lauren. A beloved nephew, as well as a son.

'I know,' she whispered with tears glistening in her eyes, slipping her arms around him, and the emotion she felt shivering through him as he pulled her close— or as close as their unborn child would allow—made her joy complete.

* * * * *

Available May 20, 2014

#3241 PLAYBOY'S LESSON
The Chatsfield
by Melanie Milburne

Lucca Chatsfield lives life by one simple motto: no rings, no strings. Adored everywhere, he's yet to meet a woman who can resist his charm. Until he's sent to the principality of Preitalle and finds his greatest challenge ever...Princess Charlotte.

#3242 RAVELLI'S DEFIANT BRIDE
The Legacies of Powerful Men
by Lynne Graham

Belle will do anything to give her siblings the security she never had. So when gorgeous Cristo Ravelli offers marriage, she won't say no. But with the ring on her finger Belle quickly discovers there's more to a marriage than saying "I do"!

#3243 WHEN DA SILVA BREAKS THE RULES
Blood Brothers
by Abby Green

Not only are Cesar Da Silva's family secrets about to be exposed... he's been caught kissing Lexie Anderson! The reclusive billionaire has smashed his own rules by romancing the high-profile actress. And judging by their chemistry this match is bound to be explosive!

#3244 THE MAN SHE CAN'T FORGET
by Maggie Cox

Gabriel knows he should walk away from Lara Bradley, and *must* show her that a happy-ever-after with him is futile. But proving just how wrong he is for her only makes him realize how just *right* she makes him feel....

HPCNM0514RA

#3245 THE HEARTBREAKER PRINCE
Royal & Ruthless
by Kim Lawrence

Forced to take a bride to avoid war with a neighboring kingdom, Prince Kamel has little patience with pampered princess Hannah, but it's his duty, and it can't be ignored. There's no love between them, but there must be heirs. And there *will* be passion....

#3246 WHAT THE GREEK CAN'T RESIST
The Untamable Greeks
by Maya Blake

CEO Arion Pantelides is always in control—but gives in to oblivion for one night with a stunning stranger...only to discover her shocking secret. Perla Lowell will show Arion she has *nothing* to hide. Until she discovers she's pregnant with his child!

#3247 A QUESTION OF HONOR
by Kate Walker

Crown prince Karim had one task: retrieve rebellious princess Clementina and return her home—pure and untouched—to her unwanted bridegroom. His honor requires him to fulfill his role, but can he resist all temptation to keep her for himself?

#3248 AN HEIR TO BIND THEM
by Dani Collins

Jaya Powers couldn't refuse gorgeous millionaire Theo Makricosta when she worked for him, and she can't refuse him now! Only this time she has a secret. Their night together had consequences that will change Theo's perfectly ordered existence forever....

HPCNM0514RB

REQUEST YOUR FREE BOOKS!

 HARLEQUIN *Presents*

PASSION GUARANTEED SEDUCTION

2 FREE NOVELS PLUS
2 FREE GIFTS!

YES! Please send me 2 FREE Harlequin Presents® novels and my 2 FREE gifts (gifts are worth about $10). After receiving them, if I don't wish to receive any more books, I can return the shipping statement marked "cancel." If I don't cancel, I will receive 6 brand-new novels every month and be billed just $4.30 per book in the U.S. or $4.99 per book in Canada. That's a saving of at least 14% off the cover price! It's quite a bargain! Shipping and handling is just 50¢ per book in the U.S. and 75¢ per book in Canada.* I understand that accepting the 2 free books and gifts places me under no obligation to buy anything. I can always return a shipment and cancel at any time. Even if I never buy another book, the two free books and gifts are mine to keep forever.

106/306 HDN FVRK

Name _____ (PLEASE PRINT)

Address _____ Apt. #

City _____ State/Prov. _____ Zip/Postal Code

Signature (if under 18, a parent or guardian must sign)

Mail to the **Harlequin® Reader Service:**
IN U.S.A.: P.O. Box 1867, Buffalo, NY 14240-1867
IN CANADA: P.O. Box 609, Fort Erie, Ontario L2A 5X3

**Are you a current subscriber to Harlequin Presents books
and want to receive the larger-print edition?
Call 1-800-873-8635 or visit www.ReaderService.com.**

* Terms and prices subject to change without notice. Prices do not include applicable taxes. Sales tax applicable in N.Y. Canadian residents will be charged applicable taxes. Offer not valid in Quebec. This offer is limited to one order per household. Not valid for current subscribers to Harlequin Presents books. All orders subject to credit approval. Credit or debit balances in a customer's account(s) may be offset by any other outstanding balance owed by or to the customer. Please allow 4 to 6 weeks for delivery. Offer available while quantities last.

HP13

* * *

"AND what about us? Where are we supposed to go?" Belle
demanded heatedly, her temper rising. "It takes time to
relocate."

"You'll have at least a month to find somewhere else,"
Cristo fielded without perceptible sympathy while he watched
the breeze push the soft clinging cotton of her top against
her breasts. He clenched his teeth together, willing back his
arousal.

"That's not very long. Five children take up a lot of
space…they're your brothers and sisters, too, so you should
care about what happens to them!" Belle launched back at
him in furious condemnation.

"Which is why I'm here to suggest that we get married and
make a home for them together," Cristo countered with harsh
emphasis as he wondered for possibly the very first time in his
life whether he really did know what he was doing.

"Married?" Belle repeated, aghast, wondering if she'd

missed a line or two in the conversation. "What on earth are you talking about?"

"You said that you wanted your siblings to enjoy the Ravelli name and lifestyle. I can only make that happen by marrying you and adopting them."

Frowning in confusion, Belle fell back a step, in too much shock to immediately respond. "Is this a joke?" she asked when she had finally found her voice again.

"It is not," Cristo replied levelly, a stray shard of sunlight breaking through the clouds to slant across his lean, strong face.

All over again, Belle studied him in wonder, because he had the smoldering dark beauty of a fallen angel. His brilliant dark eyes were nothing short of stunning below the thick screen of his lashes, and suddenly she felt breathless.

* * *

The Legacies of Powerful Men

Three tenets to live by: money, power and the ruthless pursuit of passion!

*Available in June 2014,
wherever books and ebooks are sold!*

HARLEQUIN®
Presents®

Revenge and seduction intertwine…

Harlequin Presents welcomes you to the
world of The Chatsfield:
Synonymous with style, spectacle…and scandal!

SHEIKH'S SCANDAL by *Lucy Monroe* May 2014

PLAYBOY'S LESSON by *Melanie Milburne* June 2014

SOCIALITE'S GAMBLE by *Michelle Conder* July 2014

BILLIONAIRE'S SECRET by *Chantelle Shaw* August 2014

TYCOON'S TEMPTATION by *Trish Morey* September 2014

RIVAL'S CHALLENGE by *Abby Green* October 2014

REBEL'S BARGAIN by *Annie West* November 2014

HEIRESS'S DEFIANCE by *Lynn Raye Harris* December 2014

**Step into the gilded world of The Chatsfield!
Where secrets and scandal lurk behind
every door…**

Reserve your room!

www.Harlequin.com

HP132492